Slayful Stories
Volume 3

Interludes

Melanie McCurdie

This is a work of fiction. Any names or characters, businesses or places, events or incidents, are fictitious. Any resemblance to actual persons, living or dead, or actual events is purely coincidental.

No part of this eBook may be reproduced or transmitted in any form or by any means, electronic or mechanical, including photocopying, recording or by any information storage and retrieval system, without written permission from the author .

Copyright © 2016 Melanie McCurdie

Cover image by FelRod Photography (Felipe D. Rodriguez – Photographer)
Cover model: Amanda Marie
All rights reserved.

ISBN-13: 978-1530144990
ISBN-10: 153014499X

Dedication

From Anansi Boys, by Neil Gaiman

"You know how it is. You pick up a book, flip to the dedication, and find that, once again, the author has dedicated a book to someone else and not to you. Not this time. Because we haven't yet met/have only a glancing acquaintance/are just crazy about each other/haven't seen each other in much too long/are in some way related/will never meet, but will, I trust, despite that, always think fondly of each other! This one's for you. With you know what, and you probably know why."

Those you that know me, know of my respect for Mr. Gaiman and his words. He always manages to have a quote that says it better than I ever could. There are some, however, that I wish to say thank you to personally for their contributions in making Interludes a reality.

The amazing and beautiful Amanda Marie How lucky and thankful I am to have you grace the cover of Interludes. Thank you Amanda! xxoo

To Felipe D. Rodriguez, you take amazing photos!

As always, to my family, Richard, Sam and DaveyB for being there and tolerating my creative outbursts. I love you guys.

To my sisters: you straight talkin-crazy-ass-talented ladies make me crazier and make me laugh constantly. I love you too. It's a wonderful thing to know that you have my back. Now give it back!!

To my brothers: What more could a girl need than a bunch of amazing fellas that, although you make me wonder, I couldn't do it without. Much love to you all.

Last, but never least. Muse. Thank you.

Contents

1	Visceral Kiss	1
2	Coffee and Cannoli	4
3	Bitter Violet	8
4	Serendipitous	14
5	The Jar of Self	20
6	Frozen	26
7	Snapshot	31
8	Game Night	36
9	His Ways	44
10	Coming Undone	53
11	Mourning, the Devil	59
12	The Door Face Stranger	72
13	Follow the Dog	86
	Follow The Dog: All For Beth	90
	Follow The Dog: Sterling's Demise	95
14	Bacillius Blue	101
15	Thicker Than Water	115

Introduction

Each author has a, story that stays with them, niggling and giggling in the back of their mind until it is finally, tangible enough capture and put into words. The stories that follow are all special to me for different reasons, and each was inspired by ordinary events in daily life. For instance, Snapshot was conceived while on the Ferris wheel with my sons, and Thicker Than Water was begun while drooling over photos of my dream car.

Beginning with Visceral Kiss, a romantic tale of love, loss, and revenge, I have gathered fifteen stories, three favorites and twelve unpublished and original fiction stories that will, hopefully, keep you up at night. Not to worry, there are also a few laughs and some erotic adventures to temper the terror.

I wish you a fruitful journey my friends, and may the path take you to new and interesting places.

Melanie McCurdie XO

1

Visceral Kiss

I saw him today, again. Vaughn. He should be peacefully resting in the hospital bed where I left him sated and sedated. The desire smeared smile on his face as delightful as his arousal that was still at half mast.

Vaughn said my name as I slid my red dressed lips across his hardness while he slumbered, his handsome face bruised and battered, and knuckles abraded. I could feel his hand flex, then immerse, wind itself my hair and hold me down, his hips bucking lightly when the pulsating heat filled my throat. He was always my favourite flavour.

He woke then, his resplendent eyes never left mine, just clung and tussled in the air, entrancing and hot, these visceral kisses. I could still taste passion on my tongue when Vaughn let go of my hair and growled my name in a mildly threatening way, then smiled, teeth shining sharply in the dying light. Venomously curious, I crept closer and his warm hand found my breast, his lips hard and teeth soft on my neck. I wanted to stay and never let it end, and I lost myself for a moment.

But Vaughn was distracted, too occupied to notice me reach for the syringe. My body trembled, breath gasping from the effort of controlling myself, and that's when I slid the needle home. I emptied the vial, and gave into the sensations of skin on skin. His tongue drew letters on my throat, making me shiver with regret as he fell unconscious.

Pulling me with him, he pulled me on top of him and I kissed him softly, and gasped in fear when he stiffened beneath me then relaxed. That smeared smile made him beautiful, a work of art and I left him there. That wasn't even an hour ago.

I still taste him, feel him warm against me, and its impossible but there he stands in the Lamb of God T-shirt I bought him for Christmas and those beat up jeans I can't stand, pointing to the one lighted window in the building across the street. Strains of party noises pollute the air. *No one will hear you my black winged angel* Vaughn whispers in my ear *it will be easy. I made it easy for you.*

He was right. So trusting they were, these murderers. Of course they would be; two endlessly horny teenaged boys and a woman who should know better. The baby-faced one opened the door, laughing easily at some stupid song, my stake slid as simply into they eye of the kid.

He dropped like a rock and jitters at my feet growling and snapping like a rabid dog. *Leave him like he left me*, Vaughn laughs and I fire a bullet into the forehead of the second.

The whore sits like a statue, pupils huge in the feverish light and hands shaking in supplication. Her. Her, I will make suffer. She grovels and begs with crocodile tears bubbling from her pale green eyes and steaking down her cheeks, hovering over the body of the kid whose dick she'd been sucking. I put her out of my misery.

Vaughn calls to me with his hand out, and I drop the gun, and the stake onto the horrible shag carpet. My phone rings and I see it's the hospital. I can barely say hello, trembling with regret in front of the window. The lights shatter the night, the words in my ears shatter the soul and he waits for me below. The air is heavy for a moment and I float through a flutter of vision. The world flutters, a momentary lapse and then Vaughn's hand is warm in mine and nothing else matters.

2

Coffee and Cannoli

The breakdown of monotony is the definition of loneliness. Time slides down the walls in lines of light like tears counting the hours while the world passes us by. One considers breaking the circle, throwing off kilter the delicate balance of that infinite loop, möbius be dammed - but then, the outside is a scary place and the locals have sharp teeth to match their painted claws.

For all it's faults, it also has coffee and cannoli and so the eternal struggle. Let the infernal arguments begin. Realistically, the coffee alone is worth the risk of human contact, and the cannoli is just reward for said risk. Still, I hesitate.

There are strange days afoot; the fissures that mar society's face widen with unpretty cracks that grow deeper with every amplification of stress.

A fact proven true to me just few hours ago and I recognise now that I cannot ever forget the true dangers of existence that lie beyond my front door.

Earlier this morning my cellular phone rang and I glanced down to see who was so intent on annoying me before I was caffeinated. When I looked up again, there was a man in my back yard. I know him of course. His name is William Rice and he is one of the more prominent lawyers in our city, if you consider ambulance chasing and outright prostitution of the truth. That man is the smarmiest individual I've had displeasure to meet.

Talk about self-important; Wee Willie thinks he is God's Gift to anything with a vagina and though he is hardly hideous to the eye, he practically oozes when he walks.

It'd been a while since I'd been on a date so when he asked me out last week after meeting at the grocery store, I was actually considering it until the uncouth ass grabbed my breast in the cereal aisle and kissed me like he owned me. I left him there clutching his balls and crying like a toddler on the floor. He's avoided me like the plague since, to my pleasure.

Can you imagine my surprise when William walked into view and stood in my garden? He simply stood there straight backed and boring holes in my eyes with intense observation and yet I had the distinct feeling he wasn't seeing *me* at all.

What a fucking weirdo, ignore him, I told myself, and felt the smile on the edges of my lips begin to rise remembering how we last parted ways -*Some free spirited sociopath whose chosen me as his latest victim.* I laughed as I looked down at my vibrating device.

Then he was gone.

All that I can deal with. Weirdoes are people too; as long as he wasn't affecting my life, I didn't care if he danced the rhumba down Main Street buck dressed as Jeffrey Dahmer in a party dress. Who am I to pass judgement? Whatever floats your goat and all that, but now he is back and standing much too close to my kitchen window for my taste. The glaringly obvious fact that he is nearly nude on my back lawn in the middle of the day, though upsetting, isn't my true concern. The man is evidently insane.

What gives his lack of marbles away is the ferocity with which he shouts at me about his prowess, as I've seen him do so many times on the courtroom television coverage. It's the way he punctuates his point with grunts and undulating hips while wearing a snarling smile.

It's the consistent thrusting motions he is making with amazing coordination while also continuing his other actions that is almost as disturbing as the idea that he is conducting some kind of inner orchestra.

What really drives the point home, though, is his choice of accessories. The bright white sneakers on his feet don't make quite the same statement as the ring of severed penises he is wearing around his neck or that bloody, rusty knife he is using as a baton.

I think I will forgo the coffee for today…

3

Bitter Violet

From the desk of Dr. J.T. Pasture
Re: Patient 16854-855

Dear Gentlemen,

I have observed this poor creature for several months now. I am beyond reasoning why you would insist on releasing this lovely young woman who crouches in the corner of her room and hides under the tables in the common room. The nurses have noted that should be she be pulled bodily from her hiding places, she begins rip out her hair and claw at her face. She responds to V. when the nurses come to draw blood and see that she eats, but she answers to little else. Yesterday, she flinched when I called her Violet and when the maintenance man smiled at her as he passed on his way to the kitchen.

As this is a private matter, and these words will be read only by those in charge of the hospital, I will call her V., and say that she cannot ever be integrated into society and be expected to function. Long before she came into our care, her ability to cope outside the box she was kept in was stolen away. It would be as cruel as turning a child out into the woods to survive when they have no skills to feed themselves. V's care was handed to those who run this facility and they, as we, are responsible for her wellbeing.

Gentlemen, extrapolating reasoning into emotion is such an impossible feat that we cannot stop inventing new ways to fail at it. After centuries of investigation, experimentation and the subsequent discoveries into the human psyche, we are no closer to understanding the purposes behind the whole facade of emotion. Sadly, most of those who do not express the societal prerequisite array are often labeled as psychopathic and turned over to professionals such as those involved here to house, care for and with luck, give some quality of life.

These lost souls are exposed to the limits of medical breakthrough in order to force conformation on those few who view the world differently. Have any of you considered that perhaps it's our views that are slightly skewed? It's not to say that all those who feel little to no emotion are all axe murdering psychopaths, but rather, that there is a slim margin of individuals who do not wish to cause harm. These people are, simply, unable to express such. I believe that V. is in the latter category.

If we consider the iceberg as a metaphor, could you not envision several different scenarios or alternate reasonings for certain behaviours? Perhaps, in the case of the V., we have found someone who is not unable to feel but instead, someone who has been trained and threatened into cold indifference; fear has switched her emotional thermostats to off and she is therefore unable to articulate to any degree, her thoughts or feelings towards being here.

I have wondered if she may be nonverbal and whether her reluctance to communicate is actually inability. The extreme isolation that she forces on herself seems to hint at horrors and it would certainly explain such an extreme response.

V. is naturally a loner who comes out of herself with surprising consistency to converse with her fellow patients. The time spent learning about a new friend seems to be something she enjoys and I was considering suggesting an outpatient program when she attacked Leonard Rinter with a piece of the mirror she broke in the bathroom. Thankfully, he will survive, although his vision is never going to return and nor will his ability to speak. V. has had nothing to say about the situation.

Sleep is a luxury V. rarely indulges in. I began to stagger my appearances in an effort to gauge her sleep patterns and discovered that she sleeps less than two hours per day, with several short naps throughout her 24 hours.

As V. has had no visitors in the 3 months that I have been here, she has few obvious attachments and no living beings that she seeks out that exist in life. She also has wildly romantic tendencies that seem to become more outrageous as the number of sleepless nights reach frightening levels.

As you well know, V. resists any and all medications and so the nurses, under my direction, are forced at times to place them in her foods or drinks. Quite often, after too many nights spent afraid to close her eyes, V. herself will request and take pills to make her sleep, all while begging for gin to wash it down. This is a behaviour that causes increasing concern.

V. disarmed the guard who was on E wing several nights ago, and escaped with his weapon and the keys to his truck. The vehicle was found several blocks away at a convenience store with no incidents. The guard has no lasting damage and received medical care for his injuries but up until a four hours ago, there had been no sightings or even false reports.

Tonight at 7:04 pm, a domestic disturbance was called in by a neighbour at the home of Benny Jones and we rushed to the location, unsure of what we were walking into. There was shouting that was punctuated by sharp, short screams that made me weep. Several attempts were made to ensure his safety, including two visits to the front door. One of our number lies cold on the lawn. Someone blew a hole through his chest. There is another in the local hospital fighting for her life.

The sounds of a sever beating grew worse with each interruption. I knocked on the door with my fist, calling her name softly and asked her to come out. I had never been so scared in my life, waiting for someone to answer the door and heard a roar that sent a thrill of terror up my spine. It was inhuman.

We waited, cautiously, hoping that Benny wasn't dead when the dilapidated door slowly opened and V. stepped out onto the deck wearing a soft, serene curve on her lips that could have been beautiful if she hadn't been carrying the severed head of Benny Jones and if she weren't drenched in his blood as though she's bathed in it.

Gentlemen, she is a horror dressed in bruises and battle scars, a pretty pantomime of death and she struggled little when the local law enforcement rolled up to survey the damage and lead her away. V. whispered to me when I brought her to back that she is happiest when she feels needed in some way, no matter how small it is and showed me a photo with a tiny smile that lit her eyes with less madness and more pleasure.

"I matter to someone," she murmured, holding the photo to her blood soaked chest and stared out the window at the city, "someone who doesn't see the shackles or scars."

Tonight, she smiled herself to sleep with her split lip trembling and her photo tight in her hand. I do not think she can help herself from coveting the tiny seed of knowledge that although commitment in any form is a unicorn, that there is a fragile glass spun string of emotion that connects two souls. It's not a step but a start and one I hope will be just the beginning. Only time will tell.

Dr. J. T. Pasture
Partisan

4

Serendipitous

It's been weeks since my last full night's sleep. A good night as of late is three hours without sitting bolt upright in bed naked with my hands up in defiance, and usually yelling. This morning was no exception and now I have a pulled fucking muscle to contend with. My shoulder aches and burns like a bitch and I'm expected to be sociable today. I don't want to be. I was hard pressed to even play the pretend game yesterday but my best friend, the louse, extracted a promise under threat of ... anyway, I promised I'd go and I'll follow through, under extreme duress and likely bitching and whining the whole way but oh how I hate people with a passion. I used this line of reasoning complete with examples but Lucy just laughed and slapped my ass before she slammed the door behind her. Bitch. I love her.

It was already seven am and she would be here at nine. I could be ready in 10 minutes, with five to spare but she had anticipated me and insisted that I "wear something appropriate. Put on a fucking dress. And makeup. The works."

That's when I knew exactly what she was up to. This is another dating intervention and I shudder to think what she's done to me this time. In the name of everything metal I hope it's not another one of those pretentious egotists; If it must be, I hope he is better at fucking and other indoor sports than the last one. She could at least make sure he is endowed enough to make the torture worth it, I mutter, sliding from my warm bed to my feet with a shiver. It's cold this morning.

My phone shrieks and I laugh. The ringtone never fails to amuse, and I wait til the last second to answer, hoping the caller would give up and text. They don't and I answer in a huff. "What? I'm busy." The derisive snort that answers makes me roll my eyes. "And what has you so busy? Last time I checked you were leading the bench, lady," Lucy chuckles at her own hilarity and I nod my head in agreement, and snarl in return, "If you must know, I have a tall, dark, well-hung gorgeous guy licking my kneecap as we speak. I gotta go."

"You fucking WISH! Your dildo doesn't count. Are you up? You better be in a dress. Play nice Snarla." I hated her too sometimes and affirmed that I indeed up and was wearing the silver lamée slingshot micromini that I borrowed from Kiki at the Klub. She hung up on me in disgust. I win this round.

I need to wake and bake before jumping under those delicious stinging needles of heat, and step out onto the small balcony off of my bedroom to light a joint.

In the east, the sun is slowly rising, and the sky on fire. So are my lungs. They burn, and the Herb does what it does best. I hold it while the first rays of warmth touch my nude body; exhaling, I smile and take another hit, relishing the watchful, lustful eyes of my neighbor on my ass, then my tits as I stretch and twist in a feline manner, exhaling with a laugh. My head is clearer, at last, and I toke once more before tamping it out and returning to the shower and letting the scalding water wash away the nightmare residue.

The water was so hot, nearly molten and I sighed. I was so very elevated, the sluicing of water across my sensitive nipples made them stand taut. I soaped up to a thick lather, enjoying the sensual way it slid down my skin like a lover's touch. I need to get laid. Once out of the bathroom, I stagger, the cool air like a brick wall, and wrapped in my towel, lay panting on my bed. Too warm and I tear the fluffy cotton covering off and I close my eyes. My body relaxes, almost sinking into the mattress and I feel myself drifting away. Lucy will kill me.

I'm adrift on the ocean, my mind bobbing with my breathing. It's so warm, like hellfire on my skin, and I break out in chill bumps when hands wrap around my ankles gently. They begin to inch upwards, slowly pushing my knees apart, the wetness of a tongue traces the path of the hands, now resting on my inner thighs. I couldn't open my eyes and didn't really want to. It had been so long since anyone had touched me that way, I couldn't have cared if it was a tentacle monster, as long as it continued doing what it was doing.

The hands held my thighs firmly to the bed, and I couldn't help but squirm as the tongue twisted, leaving patterns that cooled in the air. I was all sensation, writhing as the tongue stops, lingers, making me hot, beg. I'm wild for more, desperate for release, and I move my hand to rub myself. It is slapped away and I whimper, moving it back to have it slapped away again. I can't help myself and moan *Oh yes I want more. Touch me everywhere.* And then a tongue, running around and over my clit, and it feels so good that I put my hands out to pull the lips, the tongue closer only to find them restrained on the soft insides of my legs. *Put your fingers inside me* I beg again. My body shakes, craves penetration and I cry out when my right hand is released and two fingers slip easily into my pussy, and a third into my ass.

There are eyes on my face, watching me finally just give in and let the wave of pleasure overtake me. The rhythmic motion of the digits was bringing me closer, closer to the orgasm that I was desperate for. Fingers hooked into gentle claws begin to drag across the upper wall of my tunnel faster yet. *Please, please, I want to cum on your fucking hand* I gasp, needing to cum so badly but the hand stops and I'm so close to the edge, it hurts. A light laugh, male, low and full of desire whispers along my belly, turning my insides to a quivering mass of want.

I feel the fingers wriggle, stroking, fucking me again, a strong thumb on my clit rubbing and I buck my hips in time with the thrusts. I spread my legs wider, and feel my opening exposed as the warm steady pressure the head of someone's dick against my slit is turns me into an animal. I want it inside me so much that a small noise of frustration escapes. I feel the hard length of a cock sliding to me, filling me and it feels so good that I pant for air and lift my ass off the bed. It's shoved back down with the intensity of the pounding it was taking, the rigid member of a stranger slamming into my wet pussy hard enough to make my body bounce on the bed beneath me.

The electrifying sensation of a warm mouth wrapping around one of my nipples and fingers twisting the other forcefully, then harder, biting down when I squeal. Oh my pussy is wet and the stranger keeps thrusting so hard and I shout *oh fuck Fuck me,* rubbing my clit frantically. The rock hard cock deep, deeper inside my pussy and the percussive slap of his balls against my ass keep time with his grunts. I wrap my legs around his waist, attempting to pull him deeper inside me and fall over the edge of ecstasy.

Shaking from the pleasure, I feel the hardness pull out and a new pressure against my tight hole before the strangers throbbing erection is buried in my ass and his fingers are buried in my cunt, both in unison as hard as he could go. I was sure I had died and went to heaven, screaming fuck me harder and begging for more. The dick in my ass jerks and quivers, spraying my canal with hot ejaculate, and the hand between my legs keeps stabbing my pussy with sopping fingers until I soak the sheets under me again.

Then, they are gone, pulled out of me. I feel so empty. The stranger's feelers shove themselves into my mouth and I taste my juices lightly as I lick them clean. I want more and nearly cheer when they are pushed back into me with a rougher touch. It hurts now, and I don't care. It hurts so good every time the strangers knuckles slam into me that I push back against them, riding them until I explode again. I'm tired now and the hand keeps going, the mouth biting my sensitive nipple hard enough to make me shout and cum again. The stranger laughs. I open my eyes and his laugh turns into a scream. I see his face for a split second and I awake, naked and spread eagle, the sheets soaked underneath me. My phone.

"I'm on my way," Lucy bellows and jump, running to the shower to clean up quickly. My thighs ache and my pussy does too, and it makes me smile.

Throwing my hair into a loose up do, and slipping my little blue dress, I had just enough time to dash on some makeup before Lucy was bursting through the door. My nipples rub sorely against the snug fabric, pulling almost painfully as I sit in her car, perplexed, shifting now and then to relieve the pulsing between my legs. I want more of that.

The party was in full swing when we arrived. Lucy scans the room and drags me to a darkened corner where a man with a familiar face stands to greet me. He smiles at me with an almost evil leer, the touch of his hand quite familiar. Now I know it was a good idea to come after all. Now it's his turn.

5

The Jar of Self

Midnight has passed and the moon is just a sliver in the sky above her. At her feet, a man lays naked and unconscious, and she nudges his still toned ass with the tip of her bare foot. Once upon a time, Theo had brought her here, and she fell to his romantic gestures and sweeter words; granted the exotic accent probably encouraged the swoon marginally. He promised her the world, and a year later, brought her back and proposed. Happier times then, and it really wasn't so long ago that she thought that they would spend their lives together on a beach exactly like this one.

Naturally, life has had its little jokes and their marriage was no exception. It was like being promised a box of your favourite chocolates and opening it to find rotting mice, and Glory Nobel had finally had enough.

It had started 10 years ago on their wedding night, when she caught him balls deep inside her maid of honour and she'd foolishly forgave him. Tonight, she had planned an anniversary dinner unlike anything he could have imagined, down to the flowers, a decent pinot noir to go with the steak and steamed veggies she'd arranged to have served and a surprise for later.

As is always the way, the evening didn't go as Glory had planned. Theo had wolfed down the steak like some animal, looking at her only once with bloody juice dripping off his chin. Disgusting.

"I've grown hoarse over the years, trying to fix things as unobtrusively as possible. Spent forever speaking without being heard unless it suited others. Sometimes, it was so frustrating that I screamed until I fell silent, simply tired of expending useless effort. What is the point of losing my voice repeating myself? The only one getting annoyed was me."

"I'm only a vessel. Simply a jar that has finally run dry. Today, after another day of taking the brunt of more negative noise, I reached in to grab a handful of happy for myself, desperate for some reason to hold on and you.

You stood there and laughed behind your hand while I lamely tried to grasp a rainbow and instead found only crumbs.

I wonder if you know how much I hate you. You think you know, but you don't, not yet.

Pay. Attention.

The soul needs replenishing now and then. It needs to be refilled too, and though giving oneself to another is its own reward, a body requires more. It needs to feel love in return or that heart dies. It just fades away. A soul needs more than darkness and bullshit. The things I asked for would have cost nothing in monetary value, but rather a fortune in effort to show that more than personal gratification mattered.

But instead, after breaking down and showing you my wounds and thick still weeping scars, I was treated to more of the same neglectful sarcasm. Stabbing words that were thrown - they had no basis in fact - blaring lies that should the revisionist history be discarded and reality truly considered, would be plain as your forked tongue

You lying sack of shit

I've burned away so much time that can never be regained. Wasted, like the breath it's taken not to sigh and snap your fucking neck. Wasted breath and wasted words; it's all for not when the results of self-centred indifference have been slammed into your consciousness at long last

Everything is fine so long as the story suited your phantasy. As long as the tale always followed your storyline. As long as that happened, life was a carnival; except it never was. It stopped being amusing on our honeymoon. It's been a horror freak show from the get go, and payment for participating in this sick and twisted game of yours is another machete in the gut instead of a kiss and a grope at the end.

You see, nothing can be fixed when only one tries. It's hardly a relationship when it becomes about indentured servitude rather than a partnership. Nothing will change because it can't. The collar chafes - I'm not getting any younger, and frankly? I'm tired of your narcissistic crap,

What's wrong? Is a little water going to kill you?

What a pussy you turned out to be

You left me empty. The jar of self holds only air now and there's nothing left to fill it up again. It's not cracked, any more than it was before - not broken in any way, just empty. That's why we are here, or rather, you are.

Shut up cunt

Do you know how it felt, after months and years of begging to deaf eyes and to blind hearts, to be told that I was nonexistent, invisible? It hurt, a lot. It was also evidentiary proof of the suspicions I'd long-held.

Always easier to play the blame game than to admit a failing or several in your case, isn't it? Stop looking at me that way. It doesn't make my chest burst in pride to see you this way. The body I used to crave day and night, naked and shivering, bound and unable to move in the growing tide makes me happy.

It also makes me cringe because I know there's no choice really. Sad though it is, people like you never learn the easy way. No, no you don't

Now, it's time to look to the horizon and beyond. Stories end. Sometimes there's a new beginning just past one's line of sight; sometimes, like for you, it's just over.

It won't be a comfortable experience; I can promise you that, but you won't be entirely alone. I'll be sitting right up there, and my investors will be watching via live stream, right about...now.

"Good evening gentlemen and Ms. Langston and welcome. I'll be with you shortly."

Don't be rude asswipe - say hello!!

It's really not worth the struggle, you know. Sooner or later, you will get tired. Just think of the water as replenishment, and drink it down, let it fill you.

And remember how you left me empty."

6

Frozen

My nerves throb; they thrum like live wires and hurt so badly that I can't hold back the scream, but it's locked in my chest and it sits there burning. I don't know who I am, or where I am, but I know my limbs don't work and I can't breathe. I've been trying to wiggle my fingers and toes and they just don't move. The air feels warm on my face, balmy as a tropical night, like those long nights in Havana and the breeze is light and just as tasty. Why is the ground shaking? Or is it me?

Then, I remember. I know where I am and who I am. My name is Delphine Baugé and I was ice-fishing on Lac Morel just outside of town. The celebration was getting drunk and the music was fine. I recall Vetta and Jenny sharing a bottle and a kiss. Vetta tipped me a wink and a nod towards Yancy, my date, with a leer on her lips.

I remember how his eyes were a place I thought I wanted to stay. We met last week at the Marché Terra while reaching for the mangos. Two dates later, and on a whim, I invited him to join the fishing trip on the next weekend, and he agreed, to my surprise. He seemed so very much the indoor type.

My heart beats slow enough that I feel myself dying; when I revive, it palpitates painfully and thrusts a heavy thread of fear into my mind and an icepick between my ribs. Jesus what the hell...

I recall falling onto the ice. The winter sunsets are dazzling and I sat lost in Mother Nature's display, unaware of much more than the music behind me and the drunken laughter from my fellow revellers. Yancy had come behind me and placed his hand my hip and his chin on my shoulder. I was so glad to have him there, close and warm and with the sky on fire it was – it was the perfect romantic moment that I had been seriously lacking. I could have fallen.

But I fell. First onto the ice, then into the large auger hole that we had been fishing out of earlier in the day and I sank like a stone in that down parka he had insisted buy and wear today. "It will be cold and it will hardly go to waste. Come on, spoil yourself a little Delphine."

I gave in, knowing that he was likely right and still the price tag caused me to feel sorry for my bank account. I bought it though, just to see the delighted smile on his beautiful lips.

My lungs burn. They burned with some undying molten flame that grew hotter as it died, as I shrugged out of the jacket and used what little strength I had to swim upwards towards the wound in the ice. In the dying light, his face looked like heaven as he leaned down and held his hand out to pull me up with an anxious expression and a short glance around. I couldn't reach him; the water was too heavy, it weighed me down and then my lungs failed. I remember kicking as hard as I could and felt my muscles in my thighs buckle. Then, the small bit of air of been holding onto in desperation bubbled out when I screamed his name.

The world went nightmarish black and daemons danced the Yangon Swing while Mephistopheles himself jerked off above them. The dancers screamed like it was confetti on New Years Eve when he groaned and sprayed molten semen into the crowd. Never once did I dream I would find myself in Hell; I wanted out but there was nowhere to run and nowhere to step that was not coated in fiery ejaculate.

And then it was light and I still couldn't

breathe or see or move, but it was warm like comfort and then it was fire again.

Blood; it barely flows as my heart pounds harder, struggling to thaw the slush in my veins, in my chest, in my ears. Cold. I'm so cold that my lips are frozen together and I'm unable to part them to shriek for help or even to whisper his name when Yancy appears above me.

I watch with growing despair when my breath, a thin stream of vapour, hardly even colours the air under my nose. There is no strength left in my body with the elephant perched on my chest. I'm so afraid and -? Why can't I move? Why isn't he helping me?

A low humming, flies on a postulating corpse kind of sound, and the air explodes with voices and emotional distress; loud, louder, loudest. Movement and Yancy disappears behind familiar faces and starry skies. Another implosion. The elephantine pressure on my chest blows apart and I can breathe again. It is agonizing. It is bliss. There has never been a taste sweeter than oxygen and I drink as deeply as my muscles will allow.

Yancy, He is back, hovering, watching me, lowering his head in sorrow. In laughter? In some sort of dramatic fit, it seems, and he quickly glances around as a teardrop falls from his eyes onto my frozen face. ***No...no stop it! I moved!*** *I'm here.*

Why won't he help me? Dead men don't speak, I know, but I'm not dead. I'm alive and he knows it. I twitch my hand; its such an effort and his eyes narrow, the false sorrow on his face faltering. This time I jerk the old fuck finger with my Swarovski crystal skull ring on it and his eyes narrow further. Again, and once more. A smile that never reaches his eyes scorches my hope to cinders.

You know I'm here you son of a bitch god please no god please don't put me back in the dark I don't want to go back there again. "You didn't give me the chance to love you," I breathe, watching the vapour from my slow thawing lips mist the air. The sweetness turns bitter and the chilly smile just widens further, exposing jagged, rotted teeth that meshes all too well with the sound of a zipper. It breaks the sudden silence; it masks the sound of his whisper as his face disappears.

7

Snapshot
An excerpt from Autopsia

August 15, 2015
Copperton County Fair Grounds
Two hours South of Skull Creek

Sloan Wallace leans with a sigh against the chilly metal frame of the Ferris wheel, staring blankly at the group of perfectly coiffed girls that were giggling and flipping their hair as they passed. One, a willowy blonde named Marisol Bellamy, head cheerleader and biggest slut at that Sorority house she lives in, elbows her chief minion and they all titter like birds on helium. Christ she hates that sound and imagines one of the cars from the tilt-a-wheel falling on their pretty little heads.

Running the Ferris wheel is hardly a challenging activity and the only thing that is keeping her from losing her shit are the earbuds and the four hours of music she has downloaded onto her iPhone.

She yanks one bud from her ear and startles when a soft male voice says, "Hey Sloan," from her left and she squeaks in fear, caught unabashedly at her fantasy. Her co-worker and unrequited crush Dex Dane was wearing that cologne that made her want to jump him and she turns her head to find him impossibly close and smiling into her eyes. "Think maybe you should let them off?" he jokes, putting his hand over hers and pulling the lever to slow the wheel. All around them, the air is filled with the screams of the overexcited adrenaline junkies and Sloan is no longer bored out of her mind.

The trees are changing early and the colours are setting the hills on fire, sort of like a sunset on the ground. Soon it would be time to return to her final year of college and then she was off to University and seven years of brain drain. Until then, she works here at the Copperton Fair, like she has since grade ten. Dex had been here just as long and there had always been an electricity between them. The first car slows to a stop and she jumps up to let the patrons off, apologizing when the strident voice of an overprotective mother breaks through the din. "So irresponsible to have druggies running the rides!" the horrid woman's voice tremors in the late autumn air, "aren't there any wholesome kids around anymore?"

Sloan opens her mouth to tell the insipid fool that she was going into pre-med and that she could slam that in her afternoon box of Twinkies and choke on it when Dex mutters under his breath, "Like you did more with your life than suck dick and get knocked up Sara. Ignore her Sloan. Boss says we can ride for free after we empty it and clean up. What do you say? Want to ride the wheel with me?" She smiles at him and nods, and lets him get the next one, wishing absently for a mint and a brush.

Along the fence, near the garbage cans, there is a man dressed in black. She is sure it's a man and not a shadow, but observes until he wavers and dips, disappearing behind the mountain of recreational refuse. Sloan is sure she hears a muffled cry, but then the last car is ready to unload and Dex needs a hand with the drunken sot who managed to sneak a bottle of bourbon on the ride and now he's barfed all over everything. Her stomach lurches and she grabs the hose, the shadow man forgotten as she begins to wash away the used hotdogs and booze.

The water peters out and Dex takes the hose from her hand, tosses it away with a delicious smile that makes her insides flutter. He advances the wheel to number 13, her favorite one, "Will you let me kiss you at the top," he murmurs in her ear when they are seated. Sloan grabs his collar to kiss him then and there, their boss pulls the lever with a knowing laugh.

At the top, he breaks the kiss and looks around at the lights of the amusement park that glow in the sunset before he wraps his arm around her and it feels so natural that she drops her head against his shoulder. It was pretty up here anyway.

She stares up at him and embrace slackens as his jaw drops. "Sloan. Sloan look over there," and she turns her head to where he is pointing. The shadow man has company and it seems his date is not enjoying her evening from the way she is staggering. He lifts his hand and pulls her back by her long blonde hair. The woman falls back with her short dress flipping up over her hips and she hits the ground hard. The shadow man tears her clothes from her body like a child tearing a wing from a fly.

Sloan looks down and waves frantically at her boss, to no avail. He is staring at his phone with wide eyed abandon; she quickly types a text and hits send, looking back at the shadow man as he sits on her stomach hard enough for her to sit up slightly.

The light is fading from the sky and Sloan is unable to look away. "What the fuck?" Dex spits, his eyes bulging as the shadow man lifts his right hand and they see the long blade. It glistens in the ambient light. "NO! Don't!" Dex screams as the knife falls and his victim screams in a barely audible outrush, and Sloane's phone vibrates.

"Be patient Sloan. Enjoy the view and your time with Dex." She can't believe it and shows Dex the message. He curses and punches 9-1-1, rapping the information to whomever answered the call.

"Listen! There is a man stabbing a woman that he attacked behind the Fair, and he is still cutting on her! Get someone here!" The shadow man leans over her face and it disappears in his darkness. Sloan wants to go home and they are still at the top watching a something that she wishes was a fucking movie. Shadow man holds his arms up in the air; the knife shines brightly in one and his other hand has something clenched in it. She feels ill as she realizes it's the woman's face. Sloan leans her forehead against Dex's shoulder and sobs as the wheel finally begins to descend.

The police are there waiting when they get to the bottom and Sloan realizes that she didn't get her kiss at the top.

8

Game Night

Across the city, the glow of the downtown strip was starting to grow, and soon the world would come alive. He sat on the balcony wall, lost in thought. It wasn't hard to push him, to convince him that his life was a waste. He believed it already; all it took was a nudge.

I nudged him right out the large glass doors that led to the balcony. Now he's out there, sitting on the ledge with the wind tousling his hair, and it occurs to me that maybe he's aware of how he appears. Tragically handsome, overcome with loneliness, staring out into the darkness, his face streaked with tears. Oscar worthy performance. I'd give him an award if I could. If I cared at all.

I am so bored. I've taken to torturing the sheep, weeding out the ones who would provide little resistance out of sheer desperation. I have to admit though, there are some that have surprised me; their self-preservation instincts are stronger than I expected. Those I leave alone. The world is so much more fun with them in it. Still, culling the herd leaves little challenges, and as I mentioned, I am bored.

I lean nude, eating blackberries against the open glass door and observe him. He makes me hungry, but not for sustenance. Blackberries are fine for fuel, but I had a taste for something else. For flesh. Warm flesh that reacts when I bite, or scratch. Likely both. I could convince him to come back inside, let him take me and use my body, but then, the pleasure always ends too soon and then I'd have to kill him myself. I'm not that bored.

"So. What are you going to do?" I ask him from my leaning post, then pop another large, firm berry into my mouth. The tart-sweet juice fills my mouth as he startles and turns his head slowly, eyes widening as they run over my bare flesh like frisky little beasts.

I let him look, relish the feeling of his greedy stare all over my bare skin as I saunter to the nearest patio chair and lower myself, positioning my sassy chassis so that nothing is left to the imagination.

He can see everything and the rise in his pants cannot be denied, nor can the way he raptly stares as he licks his lips. "I don't know," he replies, cheeks reddening as I run the flats of my palms over my taut nipples, then lower, spreading my fingers and spreading my legs further to flick my fingers over my clit and smile cruelly.

He wrenches his eyes up at me a few times, brow furrowing in distraction, and let him suffer, then capture them at last. Holding them in my visual embrace, desiring him and still, I wonder, if I can really have my fun and still fulfil my craving. or am I barking up the wrong tree. My fingers dip into the dark cave between my thighs, enjoying the way he shifts his weight to lessen the pressure on his zipper.

"Stop." His voice is fierce and gruff, not so much pain in it now as lust. He is sweating, the effort it is taking for him to resist must be exhausting, and I respond by moaning low in my throat, and bite my lower lip. I wish it was his teeth, his fingers and the thought makes my hips buck in response. "*Dammit! Stop!*"

I don't. Should he choose to give in to his wants he'd find little fight in me, and I shift again, draping my leg over the arm so that he can see the glistening wetness and my fingers moving in and out of my sopping box.

"I'll destroy you." Curious response – A threat? Or purposeful? Foreplay? I raise an eyebrow as I arch my back, squirming with my fingers slipping deeper; His lip curves in a snarl, fingers fumbling at his clothes. One leg to the better, he swings around, the zipper opens to expose his own arousal. His hand strokes in time with my own, the tempo in unison, somewhat rougher than my own. Mutual masturbation and It feels so good.

Inside I hear a strangled cry, and rise to my feet with what feels like a lascivious smile. A louder grunt behind me when my hand pushes his away, and I drop to my knees. My captive pays no attention to our audience. She does not exist, or won't, soon. His swollen glans pushes into my warm waiting mouth and I greedily
devour it with the pleasure of a lollipop. I'd been waiting too. He fucks it like a madman, hands wrapped in my long curls, and hard enough to make me gag, gasp and lean forward for more.

Another muffled outburst inside, and a loud shatter that breaks my heart. That vase was an antique. The sound breaks the spell, his rigid member spasms on my tongue and pulls free from my lips with a popping sound as it does. Hands still in my hair, he yanks my head back hard enough to make my neck creak and I realize I may be in trouble.

Perhaps I bit off more than I can chew, and lift my eyes to meet his dark ones. He is a dangerous beast. His cock pulses hotly inches from my willing, capable lips and he stands just staring, contemplating.

I can't help myself. I wrap my slender fingers around its thick girth, and feel my inner muscles clench in want. It's no lie. Watching him from across the street in the dark while he wandered in his space naked, as he lay back and stroked himself every night. The tubal delight in my hand was something I wanted inside me, then and desperately now. I didn't care. I'd clean up the mess, if only he'd bang me like a screen door in hurricane.

More whining in the background. I hate her presence. My own hand I use to lightly stroke my clit, while he stares at me, still on my knees, his gaze skipping between my hands, his dick and the woman in the apartment. "You can't do this to me." His throat is thick with the unmistakable sound of horny, "I could snap your neck right now," he growls, hips moving in time with my tempo, and that was when he clenched his left fist hard and yanked me to my feet. It hurt so good that I came to my feet in orgasm.

"Do you want to hurt me Tom? Hurt me then. Do me like you wanted to do her," I nodded vaguely in his wife's direction, "Like she would never let you. Make me scream, if you can."

His face was close to mine, the tension palpable enough to shiver the air between us. Fingertips probe my sweet spot, teasing my entrance before smoothly thrusting up into my body. It feels too good and I make a small helpless sound, spreading my legs further and Tom takes the hint, almost violently fucking me with his hand and this time it is not some small helpless sound, but a shriek and a low giggle that I could never suppress.

My pussy is pulsing, my knees weak, and he knows it. He drags me over to the glass doors and throws me face first against them. I bounce off and back into him, my forehead bleeding from the impact. Tom is rough, pinching and biting, and I allow it, my body his to play with until later. "Look at her," he barks in my ear and I do, though my splayed hands.

Her face is pale and wan; too big eyes crowd her cookie cutter features. His hands are busy, and so is mouth; both are making my body quiver as the woman and I stare at each other through the thick paned glass. I can feel the firm head of his tool running up and down my slit, and arch slightly, hoping he will just slam it into my needing hole and stop the teasing.

The woman shakes her head, in disbelief or understanding. I'm not sure and don't care. "She doesn't want me to," Tom whispers in my ear, still rubbing against the sensitive outer lips of my sex, "I know you've been watching me. That you want this," he huffs, finally entering me with his hardness. He is much bigger than I'd encountered and my wet walls clamp down as he moves quickly against my ass. "And. You. Wanted. This," I throw back, my sentence broken by the force of his momentum. The woman watches with narrowed eyes, her expression stony.

"Yes. I did," he mutters, and I smile at her, my hands framing her face as they thud in the glass. He spits explicative after exclamation and I become sensation and experience nothing but that. I'm moving. He's lifting me impaled on his still throbbing cock to bend me over the cement wall, and the stone is painful across my skin. My ribs ache and my thighs are on fire, and he doesn't stop, only laughs low and mean in my ear. My body is shaking, quivering in throes of orgasm and pain.

I am on the precipice of madness, my sweet spot dripping and clamping down when he gave in and fills me with the fruit of his desire, and sent me over the edge again moments after. The paroxysms are incredible and I screamed when he fell on top of me, jiggling and gurgling, his softening erection still inside me, twitching. I couldn't move away and I was trapped against the cooling rock.

"He had a great ass. You have to give me that." The woman's voice. Her tone was cool and amused, even slightly aroused. The weight on my back shifts slightly then falls away, and suddenly my body is empty. I'm sore, my thighs stretched and between them, swollen and sated. Her hands run along my spine, brushing my tangled curls to the side to lightly press her lips between my shoulder blades. "Did you have fun baby?"

Standing straight with a sigh, I turn to see her close, the soft skin of her freckled cheeks glowing in the street lamps and her sanguine locks ruffled by the light breeze. Her fingers caress my scraped nipples with a pretty smile that gives me butterflies, and the touch of her tongue on them cause a different kind of tingle in my centermost place. Her hand rests on my belly, and her lips are soft and insistent, her tongue probing my lips. She leaves me breathless, and I return her fervour kiss for kiss, this time in passion and not lust when her hand finds my sperm filled cunny with her delicate fingers. She breaks the clinch, looking at her glinting hand, laughing and glancing down at the dead man on the floor, prodding him with her toe. "Next one is mine. Come to the bedroom beautiful. I want to taste him on you."

9

His Ways

Good evening sleepyhead. Don't look so afraid darling; you're safe enough, for now. Oh, I realize it's a wee bit chilly tonight but that layer of fat you've been working so hard to lose will help to keep you a bit warmer won't it? Stop the pathetic mumbling. I *have* left you dressed, after all – although that was more for my benefit than yours. I've seen your less than stellar self on more occasions than I care to remember.

I do love late spring, don't you? The scent of renewal and rebirth, the sounds of birds and bees in the trees. But of course you must, isn't that why you agreed to marry me in the spring? All the romantic gesturing and pretty words convinced me that you were *the one* and I believed you. I could never understand why you stopped using them and decided to use your fists instead.

Even after that first time, when you punched me in the back because I forgot the barbeque sauce, I was sure it was an isolated incident. It wasn't though, was it Felix?

Spring. They do so much to beautify the city at this time of year. Why, just this morning I sat right over there, sipping my coffee and watching them turn the gardens with that huge machine they keep in that shed just down the hill. But you already know that, don't you Felix? No? Lies lies lies lies lies

Felix? Honey? Shut the fuck up. I can't understand you with that gag in your mouth and I'm not removing it - so just save it. You've had your say more than once, when you thought me out of earshot. I heard you Felix. I heard you, on the phone, telling someone that you could keep me occupied for a while yet. That I was unaware of anything. Was hurting me enough to keep me distracted your plan? To hit me until I wouldn't fight your advances? What makes you think I wanted you anywhere near me, let alone inside of me after that?

Selfish son of a whore. First you withhold sex until *you* want it and then you take it whether or not I want it. If I fight, then come the fists and those are as bad as the short lived sex you crow so much about. Your fists are harder. I remember the first time you showed me your true colours.

Admittedly, I didn't see that kidney punch coming. Or any of the other ones. You didn't know that I was pregnant. I was planning to tell you with the dinner you sat at the table and ate while I bled on the kitchen floor.

Stop staring at me like you don't understand. You do know why you are here, don't you? Nod or shake your head but I expect an answer Felix.

No. No, of course it doesn't. Why would it? It never has before, even when lay there in a pain sweat and delirious from the throbbing torture that was my body begging for help. Only when I screamed and couldn't stop did you see the light.

I stood there with my hand on goodbye knowing that it didn't connect. But the words don't matter, do they? They are spent; spent and there is no return policy. I just can't be bothered to stay here and be your punching bag a moment longer. Had you stopped even once to consider that maybe I needed you?

Instead of you always being the one needing something. Anything. Everything. That maybe, maybe all the words in all the languages I possess that tell you so, are still hanging there unheard under the sound of your own wants?

It's a virtual impossibility, living as we do in a such frozen place. A narcissistic modern society with the shortest spans of attention ever recorded in human history. Oooh shiny!! I want that!! I need that!! I will kill for that. Everything in instantaneous order and yesterday at that. Gimme gimme gimme NOW NOW NOW. You're no different, and even worse.

How could you hear anything over the drone? The song of a people existing in a wanton wasteful world full of love and death and no comprehension of either. Eyes sewn wide shut. How could you possibly see past yourself? The heartbeat of a nation is all about brand, celebrity, and the newest life hack, and any action is acceptable as long as you get what you want, including murder. Read the headlines if you don't believe me.

I'd prefer that you stop struggling. You're sweating and its drawing bugs. I hate bugs. Now where were we?

Oh yes, we were discussing murder! Felix, did you know that a human being can die over and over and still live? Did you know that a soul can be viciously torn apart and still draw breath every single day?

The human survival instinct is so strong but it can be broken, with enough time and reason.

A heart can be told that it is a seed and be lulled into believing it, only to wake up buried six feet down and wondering what exactly happened.

A body can be kicked in the gut with well-meaning and absentmindedness, with neglect and lies until whatever is left of care and love and passion is frayed, filthy, spoiled and still whisper I love you. Those things hurt as much as a boot-fucking or a 150-pound sledgehammer to the solar plexus does. Those things, Felix, leave deeper wounds and thicker scars.

A body, Felix, can sit at the daily table and be assured that the meal before them is sustenance. They come back and they will sit and they will eat with a smile until they die of starvation; they return even after the discovery of the poison and still agree to another plate. Did you know that Felix? Answer me! Answer my fucking question, you son of a bitch! Maybe this will encourage you.

Great. Just. Fucking. Great. Now I have dirt on my shoes and you have a hole in your jacket. You're bleeding everywhere! I told you that I expected you to answer me.

A body can endure more than broken bones, a shattered mind and fissures in the soul that should never be.

It can, as the cliché says, take a lickin' and keep on tickin'. Humans are just fragile meatsacks but sometimes they can withstand the same pressure as coal and rarely do they shine, so covered in the soot of continuous battles. But these few are the true treasures Felix and I'll tell you why. *They can choose to survive.*

These are they equivalent of flesh cockroaches, either too stupid or too stubborn to lay down and give it up as a bad job. These are the creatures you really should be afraid of. We all should be, because no matter what you do to them, no matter how many times you step on them and grind your heel to spread their innards, they pop up like morning daisies and scuttle away to lick their wounds in the dark. Fight or flight and they choose the latter and that Felix, *that* is why they are still around to live another day.

Sweetheart, please, you're only hurting yourself. Now look what you've done; your nice new suit that you bought for the convention is all dirty and it's the last you will ever own. You look so handsome in grey and black. Do you remember that first night when you came to the performance and you were wearing a suit just like this? You told me you were in awe of my hands, jealous of the keys.

How does it feel to have your sense of touch taken away? I still have mine, Felix, but yours now belongs to the river. Now stay still and let me dust the dirt from your eyes. I swear you are such a damned child. *Hold still!* There, all better.

You see, there is always a price to pay for such survival skills Felix, something you can't comprehend because you came from privilege and so such sacrifice is foreign to you. But believe me when I tell you that something always has to suffer. There is always a cost, and sometimes, dreams just need to stay buried. Sometimes, disinterring the body does nothing more than create more questions, and unanswerable ones at that. A brain drain and about as useful as a diet team in a chocolate factory. At least there, you get some satisfaction.

Are you understanding anything that I am telling you?

No. The entirety of the human race has forgotten about its fellow bleeder - unless it's for a charitable show. The only hide worth anything is thine own. No longer is it a norm to consider one's actions or weigh one's words. Concern for the well-being of those being stepped on is little more than a media popularity contest.

In fact, the one who chooses to lift another up and walk arm in arm among the poppies with them is often kicked in the face for the effort. So why bother? Is that what's on your pathetic excuse for a mind? Why not just accept that life will never change and leave you miserable and alone?

Because.

Because *you* will never be that, not while you draw breath. Some other poor schmuck with a broken mind will come along and the cycle will start over again. Only this time the poor thing will likely die at your hands and that would be an abomination. So you see, all this is really nothing more than a public service. I don't have to lay awake at night wondering if you've finally used those fists to kill the next woman you take to our bed.

The husband of your current conquest was more than amiable and willing to assist me. I'm sure you know him, don't you Felix? The wife of your boss, tsk tsk. She screamed when she saw me sitting at her kitchen table, drinking the last cup of coffee in the house. Oh she was angry, very and demanded I leave her house until I kissed her. I understand why you wanted her now, she was quite juicy. I fucked her with your knife, by the way, with that bowie knife you stole from my dad. I found it in your drawer yesterday. They'll find her soon.

Oh, one more thing before I tuck you in Felix - I found the bottle tonight, hidden way in the back of the spice cabinet. Speaking of feeding someone poison, I do hope you enjoyed your dinner. The agony you are feeling is simply the electrical current in your veins cauterizing the hole where your heart used to be; clever, choosing a naturally occurring plant to slowly drive me off the edge.

I took it to Dr. Hottcreast, and after some awkward posturing and a little incentive, he admitted that he helped you when you came to him last week. He also admitted that he and you had become very good friends and he was happy to share the information, because you were meant to be. Soul mates. It was eye opening to know that everyone had a piece of you except me, and in light of your sexual history Felix, I count myself lucky. He told me everything, before, burying his face in my crotch and sobbing like a child. He begged me to divorce you, to let him have you. Said he loved you. I felt bad for him, Felix, terrible for assuming the next soul you sank your claws into would be female. I killed him, out of pity and disgust. Stop screaming.

What's wrong Felix? You didn't mind sharing his bed did you? To hear him tell it, you downright loved banging him every night back here. This card he showed me says, "My darling Harold, I can't wait for this weekend and to spend forever in your arms." Why are you crying Felix? I thought you wanted to spend eternity together? Now you can.

10

Coming Undone

Folklore and childhood tales vary from family to family and certainly in this case it is no different. Those dark tales told by firelight sometimes become tangible and the unknown becomes frighteningly real. For 30-year-old Dee Carpenter, it is a perfectly warm Saturday in June. Dee and her live in boyfriend are celebrating her birthday in the backyard with friends and family.

a bright kitchen - a small dog scampers into the room with its nails clicking on the tiles. -laughing and party sounds from outside - classic rock music. Small dog sniffs along the floor and growls at the window when a shadow passes by. On the counter a black cordless phone begins to ring. The handle of the door rattles slightly and stops

Francis: And where are you going birthday girl? Come on Dee, you promised. No calls til tomorrow. Francis: (con;t) You're always on the damned phone. Don't roll your eyes at me.

Dee: (annoyed) You just love to torture me don't you? It could be important, like the that guy in scary movie calling to save me from you.

Frances: (with a nasty laugh) You wish it was, and you love it. Come on honey. Just for a few more hours okay? Everyone came for you, not to see you on the horn.

Dee: Fine. But it's your fault if I die.

*inside - answering machine interrupts *

Dee's Voice: **(in weird voice) Greetings Earthlings! I'm out of my mind right now, and Francis isn't far behind.**

Are you sure you couldn't have texted instead?
giggle do whatcha gotta! Ciao! **answering machine beeps. a gasp and a woman's shaky voice**

Cora: DEE? God Dee, I need you, please pick up? Jesus...
click and hiss of a lighter followed by a shaky inhale

Dee: It's Cora. (*coughing fit)* Fuck me I gotta quit these things. Okay, *I* know it's been a while so don't be hard on me. I emailed you on Friday so you can't complain too hard. Dee, please pick up the phone. Something's happened. I'm not sure exactly how explain it and I could and will call back to explain, if I can, but you need to know that I put this in a letter and sent it to you.

I may not be able to call if - This needs to be in writing. It's going to sound nuts, like you expected any less, but I mean really nuts and it's true. I swear on my life it is. On my own grave even.

drinking sound - wheeze and cough from Cora

Cora: I really wish you had answered Dee. I'll call back later, if I can. I love you Dee. Happy Birthday.

call disconnect - dial tone

outside - Dee - NO DON'T YOU DA- *a scream, a splash and laughter*

Unknown Female voice: Francis ain't getting any tonight for that *giggle* She loves that dress.

Inside - Dog barks and howls at the door. Scratches and whines in a fretful way.

deeper in the house - slamming door - soft dark chuckle - dog whines louder

Break in the music - Phone rings three times -

Francis' Voice: **(deep) You've reached Francis and Deidre. Dee can't come to the phone right now. I have her tied up in the basement... (muffled noise) Just kidding! We're busy. You know what to do (evil chuckle) Coming dear!**

Cora: For fuck sake, can't you two do anything normal? Dee, it can't wait and you need to pick up the phone! This is so frustrating! (growls) You know that story mum used to tell us about Gramma and Great-Gramma and so on? About how they all just fell to pieces and died too young? I'm hoping against hope and praying you remember or I will sound well and truly bonkers. I'm not convinced I'm not crazy.

I never believed a word of it you know. Not even that first time. Do you remember? We were maybe four or five and mum had invited you for a slumber party. I know Aunt Cate hated that Mum loved all that scary stuff but for some reason said yes when mum called (laughs sadly) usually it was a big old **Hell NO**! Anyway, it was right near Halloween and the house and yard were decorated with pumpkins and zombies and those fuzzy bats she hung from the trees. *amused chuckle and inhale*

Francis: *opens door* I'm just going inside for a second! (muffled voice) I need to get more beer! Okay Mom okay, I'll go through the garage. 27 years old and I still get told what to do by my mother - yeah yeah I'm goin!

Cora: Mum let us help make rice Krispy squares in her coffin tin and we decorated them with bones and flowers. You were so scared of the bones.

Anyway, that night mum lit the fireplace and we gorged ourselves on sweet stuff while she told us that story.

It was little more than a delicious wasn't it? Knowing your mother would disapprove, and somehow that made it even scarier. Dee, WHERE ARE YOU? God. *sniffling* I need you. I'm scared and I need you.

I just didn't believe it when my mum told me about how all Alexander women, what were the words, "come undone and die on the floor." It's creepy as fuck and dammit Dee- *where the hell are you*?! *quiet sobbing* The one time I really need you and —

Francis: (still outside) Okay Mom okay; I'll go through the garage. (to self) 27 years old and I still get told what to do by my mother - yeah yeah I'm *goin*!

*Cora: *loud rattling in the background** (scared tone) What the hell is that?! Dee, honey, I'm sorry to call today with this but mum's gone. I found her tonight when I came round to bring her dinner. She'd been wearing a bandage on her ear for a few days and she just wouldn't talk about it. She wouldn't let me look either. I was going to force her to come to the doctor with me this morning. She was fine when I arrived; she had made me my favourite breakfast, from when I was five, and reminded me of that story.

She seemed fine otherwise but that bandage was bothering me and when I told her about the doctor she ripped off that thing and *a scream followed by choking sounds and heavy breathing -a trembling breath*

Cora: **OH FUCK DEE!!!**

dial tone

11

Mourning, the Devil
This is the manuscript for Mourning, the Devil.
Coming soon to The Carmen Theatre Group

I have been in mourning too long. So much time wasted bemoaning a life that could never have happened. Not in reality and certainly not now that I can see how the world truly is. Misery loves company. It is no lie, because I would rather be miserable with people all around me than to be miserable on my own. I am what I am. *Do not misunderstand.* That was not a slip of the tongue. *What* I am. I am a thing. A freak of nature even and though many would consider the terms derogatory or self-depreciating, I consider them apt.

I cannot take responsibility for how I began. That was beyond my control. Many scoff and debate nature versus nurture, but I was not a hard-hearted monster before that day.

Once upon a time, as they say, I was not this.

Until then I was not in command. I came to a state of cognizance and was swept away by a tsunami of darkness and given a gift in an epiphany, a sudden understanding of what I was. At that instant, my actions were, without doubt, firmly in my grasp as they are now.

I am responsible for the deaths that occurred in that derailment last week. It was a mistake on my part to let that one escape. I am sure their families will mourn much as I have and I offer my sympathies. Mourning is hard work. As to those who were destroyed, collateral damage and par for the course. It's not cold, exactly. Its business. Shit happens, sometimes it's unfortunate but it does nonetheless and so it has been for as long as humanity has existed.

"What happened to you? How did you become what you are? What are you, then?"

Ugh. They are mere speaking vermin and now one is speaking to me. Some poor creature forced into the woods to feed itself, and for all intents and purposes, alone. There are worse eventualities. "What happened to me? How did I become this?" I wonder if it has the capability to understand and probe its mind to test its defenses and find immediate obstacles. Very unusual in its kind. More unusual is that its mind pushes back. Less rare is that it recoils.

Perhaps one day I will find one that doesn't. Still, the idea, like a seed, once planted will grow and my memories resurface easily.

"In my youth, the Before, I lived what seemed a fairy-tale life. I know now that I was sheltered and it is both a blessing and a curse to be aware of it. Memories of the Before are happy and carefree, with no tears or terrors. We kept residence in a rented home far from the draw of the cities. A sprawling acreage with wildlife, surrounded by trees and gardens and grounds. When I was but a babe Mother and I would wander picking wildflowers and chasing butterflies but we never went into the dense forest that ran along the end of the property. Mother always said the shack was the last chance to stop. It was there, in that intensely interesting and forbidden place, that Father hunted for food in the fall.

We also had stables and several docile horses and so in the summertime Mother and I would ride while she gave me the lessons Father insisted I continue. When winter came we built snowmen and told stories by the fireplace while I sipped hot cocoa. There were many years there was heavy snow and as there were no close neighbors, we were often alone the three of us for weeks without power. My father always made sure we had enough wood to last us a month, should the weather turn against us and he never failed to calculate just right.

Mother kept us fed with a never-ending parade of delicious meals and her bright eyes. The best part of that time is memory of Mother's rich singing voice; that familiar melody brought us through so much. Father often said she was a witch and Mother would blush and laugh like a young girl. Father would shake his head with a smile and he would cup the curve of her face with his hand before he'd dip to kiss her lips. They loved each other.

The only mar in the perfection was the Preacher. Once a month God's Messenger, as Father titled him, would come, and oh, oh I despised that man when he read out of that ridiculous book he carried like some talisman. Often I would overtly observe his eyes tracing the lines of my mother's breasts as she bowed over her bible, or on her behind in those horrible clam diggers she insisted on wearing. He even went so far as to stroke her nipple through the thin t-shirt she wore on that last visit while Father was lost in his prayers. I haven't forgotten.

Father went Home on my sixteenth birthday. He had been laying by wood for weeks and Mother had been so distant that he began going further out into the property to cut. Often he wouldn't return until after dark, and he was always dragging a load of wood behind him. That night was the same as it had been for far too long. Father appeared at the edge of the nearest copse, hauling a larger than usual load.

He looked up to see Mother standing at the window and the oddest expression blanketed his face. I remember yawning. The sun had set barely an hour before and the sky was still fading to black. Mother still stood at the window, now with her chest heaving and staring out the window at Father redoubled his efforts and was moving again.

With her back to me, Mother told me to finish my milk, then turned with a sly smile and offered that if I did so quickly, I would receive an extra cookie. Mother's cookies were the best in county and so I drank the lukewarm liquid at a gulp. There was some sort of grit at the bottom of the glass that tasted strange and it made my tongue numb. When I complained, Mother poured more milk into the glass without a word and swirled it around a few times like they did in that book I was reading. She said it would wash the bad taste away. She was right. She placed an extra cookie in front of me that I snatched up like a child and she laughed, told me to eat my cookies and while I did she told me a story to pass the time.

The story was about a girl who lay sleeping in the forest, her body offered as a sacrifice to the monster that lived in the woods. Mother smiled knowingly; she told me about how the girl dozed while her maidenhead was stolen and how she was revered for saving her town.

I felt very uneasily sleepy and Mother laughed, promising to save me a cookie until tomorrow, then helped me to the bedroom with reassurances that it was just a story when I asked her why she chose that tale then fell dead the moment I hit the mattress with my face turned towards the window and the woods beyond."

The human has come closer in my reminiscence, much to my dismay. The curse of being lost in one's head was the opportunity for the wildlife to invade your space; much to my chagrin,
this vermin was not unattractive. It wouldn't do to allow more but its closeness is somewhat of a relief. I will never forget that night and it leaves me colder than usual to recount it.

"I could hear Father cursing and grunting, speaking words that were somehow appropriate in their profanity. I was not afraid but rather aroused and I slowly opened my eyes to stare out the window at the fire that burned briskly not far from the shack. Once we kept chickens there until the foxes and other creatures killed them all. Father was tussling with a buxom brunette while Mother stood nearby with her mouth hanging open, silent, but her eyes screamed until they vibrated.

Mother had told me that story for a purpose. I knew it the moment she snapped her mouth shut and glued her eyes to me as I crept from the house. Father was shouting at her in an impatient whine, "Yessa! Will you move your fat ass and help me before this bitch wakes her!?" he huffed in frustrated tone. Mother shook her head slowly back and forth, backed away and tittered her insane little laugh when I flew between them and knocked the struggling bombshell to the ground.

Father covered his eyes and sank to his knees muttering something akin to a prayer. I told him to run and he just got louder so I silenced his curses with a backhand. Mother ran to his side, as I predicted she would. It didn't matter. I flicked my eyes to her groveling in the dirt with Father's head lolling to in her lap and the meanness that I found raging there was both familiar and a comfort.

The bombshell had begun to shiver in the grassy area near the shack, her full breasts jiggling with nipples peaked in the night air. She smelled of pure driven snow under that gaudy perfume the thought was sophisticated; that mist she sprayed on her bare skin, dreaming of how it will be on her wedding night with a stardust smile. But at that moment, her large ocean colored eyes widened when I turned my full attention to her and her perfect cupid' bow lips trembled.

She was perfection in fear, the way every muscle

thrummed with the rapid intake of breath. Such a sweet sacrifice and a virgin no less.

I knew her well. This was the daughter of that damned preacher that came once a month to pray over our home. She flirted and fluttered around Father like a hummingbird on crack and I hated the air that she breathed. Mother was always nervous on those Sundays and was up at dawn baking for them.

They never partook of even a crumb of her hard work, especially the bombshell. That tight little smile she gave Father when he handed her tea in the chipped china, as though it were beneath her. That bitch had no idea it was the best dishware in our home, and it was saved for *her*. I hated her with furious delight.

The man I called Father was moaning and crawling on his knees, begging me to stop and leave her alone. His well-loved voice was just a mindless buzz in my ears. Only I mattered now and the vermin that infested this place would feed me well. Still I understood the premise and shuddered when his warm meaty hand touched the hem of the light shift I wore. He choked out the only word that made sense to me; Devil and it lingers in my ears like an echo. Mother had disappeared while my attention was elsewhere, running off in fear as was the norm.

Both my parents were no more than sheep that avoided confrontation like the plague. I tore my father's face from his skull and it gave easily with a wet tearing noise when it finally came free. He flailed and cried like a wounded puppy, his heels pounding divots in the dirt while his hands traversed the air around his head.

The bombshell wailed in terror when Father found his feet and gibbered into the night air. Her eyes grew still larger while Father tore his own eyes from his head and dove directly into the briskly burning fire. The air smelled like Mother's Friday roast. I peeled my nighty over my head, and exposed my well-earned supple form in the flame light. Bombshell saw me then, what I am under this flesh mask. She tried to run.

I was stronger then and I admit, the first glimpse of the homemade contraption I'd fashioned from the oak leavings Father had lying around in his workshop was more than sufficient to solicit fear. It fitted snugly around my hips, held tight even when she tried to claw it from my skin in some misguided effort to stop me. I laughed when she shrieked, laughed harder when I felt her hymen break and fucked her as though her life depended on it when she begged for mercy. Her blood stained the head of my nail-studded appendage, turning the brightly shining points into scarlet covered jewels.

I could see them when I pulled back from above her to watch it disappear and reappear between us with bits of flesh falling from the points.

Bombshell clawed at my face and I bit her breast hard enough to tear a sizable chunk from the softness, then slammed my hips with gusto into her body. I only wished I could fill her full of my seed but the expression of horrified desire was enough to make me cum nonetheless and I groaned with pleasure when she went limp.

Not dead yet. I had plans for her end that would make her Daddy shudder in shame. Mother muttered behind me and I turned towards her with my cock dripping gore. She gasped and turned away with the color draining from her face, her slight shoulders heaving. Bombshell was gurgling my name in a guttural drippy tone and the sound of her voice pleading irritated to the core.

Her hair was soft as silk in my fingers and twisted like a coarse rope in my fist. I couldn't have cared who heard her splutter and choke when I thrust my tool into her open mouth and Hell help me, my cunt was dripping when the warmth of her blood splattered my thighs. She beat at my thighs ineffectually, her whole body trembling while I forced her to deep throat and it felt great to feel her blow hot air through her nose in an effort not to die.

I let her fall away to succumb or survive long enough for me to have further way with her luscious and full hide. Her face was ruined, no longer the entirely innocent Barbie doll. Her once perfect cupid lips hung in strips of dripping flesh, as did the ones between her splayed legs."

"So you fucked the preacher's daughter with a strap-on. That doesn't make you a Devil. That makes you kinky. Doesn't she have a name?" Humans.

"Yes she had a name. Her bible thumping Daddy named her Virginia. Ginny. Why does it matter so much what her name was?

Father was still jitterbugging in the fire, though thankfully his agonized squalling was brief. Now he was blackened and too spoiled to do more than feed the animals that lurked in the dark underbrush. The bombshell, however, still had plenty of creamy nubile meat on her bones and though she drooled gore, she is still the one I cannot forget. I dreamed of destroying her so many times and woke soaked in sweat and cum so often that it seemed almost unreal. Father couldn't have chosen better.

Bombshell had found her feet and was tottering into the deliciously dark forest with blood and bits of tissue sliding down the insides of her thighs. I called her name like a kiss on the heavily scented air and she squeaked, scuttled off like a terrified rabbit into the trees. The thrill of the hunt electrified my nerve endings was only kindred to ecstasy and with eyes closed I followed her into the dense foliage.

Hours later or days perhaps, I came back to myself crouching in the long grass on the edge of civilization and covered in blood that didn't belong to me. Father's body was gone from the still warm ashes in the fire pit. His watch still lying in the embers, the leather band burned away and the face cracked and charred. Mother was singing that same familiar tune in the kitchen. She had the windows open and the fragrance of fresh baked apple pie teased my nostrils and turned my stomach slightly. I was very full, reeked of dead leaves and humanity and really just wanted a shower. I crept closer, my ear and eyes on the snaking road that lead to our home. We were about to have company and I was a fucking mess, not to mention covered in evidence.

Mother appeared at the back door and scanned the trees presumably for me. "Lila," she called, seeing me despite my cover, "come in darling." She wiped her hands obsessively on the pristine white apron she wore and waved me forward. I should have known she would spot me but had hoped she wouldn't.

Nude, I stepped from my camouflage and relished the wince on her face when she finally took in my crimson coat. Her trembling hand hung in the air and she smiled when I took it gently. "Come my beautiful girl," she whispered in my stinking hair, and then a vicious little smirk slithered across her lips, "come my sweet child, the Preacher is coming soon. Aren't you hungry?" I hadn't been but at her suggestion my stomach grumbled and I smiled in agreement.

"And so why haven't you killed me yet?"

Mother appears in the shadows, her black eyes glimmering as she watches my hand stroke the stubbly cheek of the impertinent vermin, and they narrow when he makes his move as was predicted. Humans are nothing if not that. "Because I want you to fuck me," and his eyes widened with his smile, "and then I have a special job for you."

I allow him to use my body, after all its little more than a fuck in the woods in order to gain so much more. The important thing lies inside. In my belly. The beast that I carry cries for blood and I will provide for him as my Mother has for me.

12

The Door Face Stranger

It is 5 am and I am still awake. This makes three days now. No. Five....six? Forever. I hate this room, it smells like death and despair. I'm sick. Physically I am failing; this morning my hands were full of hair and I can't eat without feeling queasy. I wasn't mentally ill before I arrived but I am now. Exhausted to the point of delirium and still my mind won't shut off, the voices won't stop nattering long enough for me to rest.

I can't write, the one thing that kept the crazy at bay, and they took my papers and pens away when they stuck me in this forgotten hell - trapped me in here after I opened my arms to release the pain with my blood on the walls. I can't think anymore, not with all the little pills and needles they keep giving me. I hate them. The needles make my skin crawl and ache and I heard Nurse Noxious say during her last torture session that my veins were shrinking.

When I turned my head she was staring at me with a smug smirk rippling on her livery lips. I'm afraid of her.

The only sight I get to see outside of these walls is the hallway when they drag me out of my personal purgatory to the exam room. I fight every time and every time she turns up the meanness a little bit more; the sadistic horror show of a human enjoys every second of it. My arms are riddled in bruises and holes as though I've been mainlining my entire adult life but I have never touched anything stronger than the occasional glass of wine. Nurse Noxious kept running her hand up my thigh as I lay there restrained. Her rough fingertips brushing the soft pubic hair that they refused to let me shave with that ugly smirk on her uglier face, while her assistant stabbed me again with that needle. I don't want to think of her anymore.

Soon I may shut down, or shut off completely. If only I could get to something sharper, and long enough to ram into my eye or perhaps cut my throat with. Much longer in this hell I might rip my eyes out with my own fingers. There is never enough time to react and escape. I have attempted that. Twice. Now they are wise to me. The lunatic ravings play over and over in my head, laughing at me for thinking that just this once someone didn't want to hurt me. *Stupid girl why don't you DIIIEEEE* they shriek and I howl along. I just need sleep. A few hours of rest will make the imps in the shadows go away.

I can keep the voices quiet, even stop them if I don't swallow the pills. I have a collection now, hidden here where they will never find them. I beat at my already bruised temples in an effort to jar the crazy loose. maybe drive it out through my ear, and only succeed in splitting my already bleeding lip and making my head throb.

Out. I *want* OUT. God, let me out or strike me dead but make it end. I miss my life. The voices only grow louder, more jeering and I whisper back - I know. *I KNOW!!* I wish they would stop telling me. I know it was a lie and that I am stupid. I regret it my actions every second of my life but the monsters that work here, they turn their heads away when I attempt to refute their claims. I claw constantly at my face with my fleshy fingertips. Nurse Noxious clips my nails almost too short, a safety precaution she says.

The hospital staff peek through the tiny glass square in the door, making notes and nodding to themselves in that pretentious way the overeducated have. They always wear the same smug masks with too bright eyes and a healthy outside glow. I haven't been outdoors since the day I was brought here. I hate them too. The expression in each pair of eyes I see paints me with the same brush, the same assumptions made out of habit rather than choice; because it is expected to agree. Not one time has someone spoken *to* me rather than at me, instead they throw labels and judgments. Clinically insane, dissociative, violent, they say, a dangerous killer.

I am none of those things, except a killer, and not dangerous at that. I keep trying to explain it to the doctors. I kept telling them it was in self-defense, that I had no more choice then than I do now; much less now with the chemicals fogging my thoughts. I didn't want to kill them. I had to do it. I *had* to.

There is a new face in the hole. A shiny new mask sent just to confuse and confound me further. Its eyes are dark and deep, thoughtful as they observe. The voices quiet some, the drop in volume from screaming to a dull roar, all of them muttering about this new one.

We could kill him they murmur, skittering away into the darker corners, *we could **fuck** him* they giggle like teenaged girls. **Behave** says the Mother and they hush. It is quiet in the room and in my head as it's brown eyes observe me on my knees in the corner with as close to no expression change at all. Even the human masks show some pity, at some stage. Perhaps it is not human.

Curious, the monsters creep back into their holes and crypts, waiting and watching for Mother as they plan their moment to attack. I do not want to hurt anyone. I just want out of this place. I fight not to drop my head in shame and see my vision blur and sting. The face smiles, fiercely, gently, his eyes saddened at what they see and I am suddenly shy and shattered with no place to hide. I am not crazy. I am *not*, and I can't hold his gaze to defend myself any longer, not so exposed as I am and so I look away, shivering in my misery.

Killer they sing, as the new face pulls away, *Idiot!! Did you think he'd want to save YOU? Who would want you?* and my tears fall, scalding my already flushed face. Someone must have, once upon a time. The voices stab me over and over, their words honed to destroy me. They leave bloodless wounds behind, stabbing until I sob, and even then I am unable to even raise my hands in a makeshift mask to cover my pain. I just don't have the will to try. *He's back*, the voices marvel and I drop my head lower. His gaze weighs so heavily on my bones.

"Please stop staring."

My voice is little more than a gruff whisper as I haven't used it except to answer the occasional demand or to scream when I am strapped to that damned table in the exam room.

I am dead inside, little more than a ghost but I manage to muster what little backbone and humanity I have left into my plea. There isn't much, voice or humanity, and I'm so tired of looking at these filthy floors under my too pale knees. Filthy knees. I don't remember the last time I felt clean and certainly the tangles in my hair attest to the time that has passed.

The weight of his stare moves away and my lungs explode in a harsh exhale, surprising me into tears again. I wasn't aware that I'd been holding it and that frightens me more than the clicking of the key in the lock.

My breath comes quicker, my eyes still downcast. I can see the door sweep open, the little rubber flap at the bottom frayed like teeth that catch the dust on the mats and drag it along in a visible arc. A pair of highly polished shoes step towards me and I catch my breath again. The Imps startle and shriek, forcing me to skitter away before the shoes can reach me. The last time they got too close and I was unable to walk for three days. The last time I bled for three weeks. They slow but do not cease, tentatively creeping closer and closer. I have nowhere to go. I am rapped like a rat in a trap and all too aware of it.

"Should I come in too sir?"

A voice from the doorway. One of the guards. He is not a kind person, one of the mean ones and I skitter further backwards. I was in trouble when my back hit the wall. All I have left is my fingertips and I press them into my eyes.

They softly move with the pressure, spreading out like the sugar cookie dough we used to make at Christmastime. I increase the pressure softly, at first, then harder. The pain is explosive and my tortured sockets leak down my face. It hurts so badly but be damned if I am going to live through it again. I would rather die by my own hands.

My wrists are smothered and pulled out and away, and I fight but they are held tight to my sides. "No no no no **NO**!!!" I scream and the livid voices are screeching along with my frustrated wails and I throw my head back. Last resort. Last chance. "STOP," a firm male voice barks and I throw my head forward with all I have and feel his nose crack under my forehead,

His grip tightens on my arms and I try again, my forward momentum stopped as I open my eyes and see the thick blood that is flowing from his nose, turning his mouth and chin red. But that's not why I stopped.

Officer Unfriendly has joined the party. His gun is drawn and pointed directly at my temple. I can feel the cold metal pressing hard beside my left eye, see it gleaming in the natural light that is flowing through the open door. Its eye is frigid as I stare into the eyes of the Door Face Stranger. My chest moves rapidly, I can't breathe, my fear bigger than I am.

The barrel tip presses harder still and my heart stops, staggers, beats. All I can do is hope that one of them will end my misery. Just kill me and let me rest. The voices keep blaring in my head *DO IT DO IT DO IT* they scream *end it kill her she deserves it.* Mother has no authority now that the riots have begun.

"Kindly go back to the doorway and put your gun away for Christ's sake."

"But, sir, she's a dangerous offender. It's my JOB!!"

"You'll be jobless shortly Mr. Duncan..."

The pressure on my temple eases, then vanishes, as does the elephant that had been sitting on my chest. I'm horrified as an acrid smell assaults my sinuses and I sob in self-disgust. In my fear, my bladder has let go and the last of my self-worth drains into the puddle of urine beneath me. I am less than a shell of a human now. How I wish I could just fade away.

A gentle hand strokes my hair and I stiffen in surprise, the hand that was once on my right wrist. My arm is free. His other now strokes my back in a gentle motion. It's been forever since anyone touched me, and I give up, give in and silently cry.

"It's over now. All this humiliation goes away right now. It never existed."

Lies. Lies and more lies and the door is still open and I'm frozen in the arms of an unfamiliarly gentle man. A Stranger. My way is clear. It's right there and I just can't move away. The monsters are confused, whining at each other from their destructive activities.

Mother paces, fingers behind my eyes digging into my will and urging me to run, crawl, TRY. I want to obey. I want it badly enough that I can smell the rainstorm that was raging outside the windows on the other side. I want out of this piss smelling room and in the fresh clean air. I want to let the rain wash the stench of this place away. I want that so badly that my legs are trembling as they try to lift me and fail. Of course they would.

I was forced to swallow the noontime drugs. Nurse Noxious stormed into my room carrying the small paper cup that held the pills and with her was Officer Unfriendly.

He kicked me hard, knocking me on my side then pulled me to my knees by my hair, his big hand releasing it and then cutting off my air while shoving his thick rough fingers inside of me. I had no chance to scream. He fucked me with his hand, while pushing the pills into my mouth with his other;

he blocked my mouth and nose and I had no choice.

Once I had swallowed the damned things, he yanked his fingers out of my violated pussy and shoved me face down to the dirty floor. I tried crawl away, but he held me fast and shoved his cock in as far as it would go. It hurt and I screamed at last, loud as I could and that's when I saw stars. I'd forgotten Nurse Noxious. She laughed and encouraged him to pound harder. I came out of self-defense. It wasn't out of pleasure, or worth the further injury to continue to fight. Thankfully he pulled out this time and spared me the added stress of worrying that I may wind up pregnant in this place.

"Can you walk?"

Walk? I can't even speak or lift my eyes, unable to articulate more than a bare shake of my head. That was enough it appears.
"Mr. Duncan? Where is her room please?"

Officer Unfriendly steps over the threshold and the panic rat starts to gnash in my belly. The voices clamor in alarm but I can't move or protest, only lift my eyes to plead, and I do. I lift them to the stranger whose arms are still around me and beg. I have no one else.

Mother snaps and the bells cease, all monsters to shelter. The stranger smiles into my desperate stare. A smile that doesn't quite meet his eyes, and one that stiffens the small lines around his mouth and creases his forehead creases his lips and he snaps at the guard in a growl. "I didn't say come in. I asked where her room was."

"You're standing in it. Sir. After the last time she decided to cut herself open and draw in her own blood on the walls, they put her here permanently. She isn't right, sir." Officer Unfriendly's tone jeers from the doorway, finding my discomfort amusing. I look to the wall and see the tiny scratches I'd made there with a small stone that fell on my head in the night. I remember the first night I made my mark. Small enough not to be noticed, deep enough to remind me of the eternity of darkness I had already been mired in. The stranger looks as well, his breath catching in his chest and I watch his eyes crawl over the notches in the padded covering with disbelief and horror.

"Four months. You've kept this woman here in this room for four months? This isn't for her safety. This is cruel. Find me a room *now* Mr. Duncan, and gather her belongings," the Stranger snapped as he held his hand out to me, "Come, let's take you home."

I hear the words.

They bounce off my mind, ricocheting against the others that had been drilled into it since I cut the throat of the first. Murderess. Insane. For life. Killer. KILLER. But home. I have no home. Not now. I am undoubtedly unwelcome, as I've been alone since they dragged me shackled through the doors. Not a single visitor save the Door Faces and this Stranger. I can't move from my wet spot on the floor and I look at his hand for a long moment before raising my gaze to his face again.

"Where is home?" I ask softly and his only answer is a vague smile and a brush of his fingers across my forehead. His touch stings my skin as he sweeps the matted hair from my face and frowns at the reddish purple bruising that is hidden under it. The rattling clatter from the doorway startles us both, and the Stranger takes a deep breath and exhales with a rapidly cooling warmth in his expression. A wheelchair that looks older than Christ with Officer Unfriendly at the controls, his knuckles white and trembling slightly on the handles as he glares at the stranger.

"Please, don't let him touch me." My voice, already rough from disuse cracks further, fracturing my words before they reach his ears and I try again. This time I succeed.

The Stranger's eyes narrow, considering me at his feet, and rises with a stony expression replacing the kinder one. From human into something not remotely so and it should scare me, but I am not afraid. It is familiar and I feel safe. All I can do is watch from where I wait, my legs beginning to tingle slightly. I hope he hurts him.

"Mr. Duncan, if you please, I'll take the chair now." The stranger's words, though mild, contain a threat that Officer Unfriendly is clearly missing. The monsters snarl when the guard's features become more predatory than professional and he continues to destroy me with his open glare. It doesn't last long.

The Stranger speaks to him sotto voce, his hands casually in the pockets of his trousers and demeanor far less so. Officer Unfriendly's eyes snap to the Stranger's, bulging slightly and jittering when the intent is realized. A fine sheen of sweat covers his creased forehead. He is afraid. "Do you understand me Mr. Duncan? Nod if it's clear, but I expect an answer."

Officer Unfriendly's eyes get so large they look as though they might pop out if his head and I watch with amusement as a dark spot appears at his zipper and spreads rapidly. The tingling in my legs is stronger, as is the desire to close my eyes and escape this mess so strong that my vision wavers like the road on a hot summer day.

"Yes sir Mr. Zachary," he stammers, hands dropping to cover his crotch, and his face blazing red and dripping in embarrassment. He nearly runs down the hallway in his efforts to get away. Zachary. So the Stranger had a name and a temper it seemed.

I wonder if this experience will change Officer Unfriendly, or will his fear make him worse. If is for the worse, I will give him a reason to kill me.

My eyes keep closing. I just can't stay awake and I am afraid to fall to sleep alone. The door is still open. It shines like heaven, the sun so strong on my face that I can feel it baking off the depression and tombstone mentality. His arms are so strong when he lifts me from the floor and I cannot struggle anymore. My head falls to his shoulder as the darkness takes me. Maybe I will wake up in a better place, maybe I won't wake up at all. All I had to go on is that I was out, and this Mr. Zachary was taking me home. The rest I will trust to fate.

13

Follow the Dog

We followed the dog. It was so cold and damp, and the night pitch black. We were supposed to land in warmer climes, and dressed for arrival, not for snow and temperatures below zero. I have no idea where Jack has gotten to. One minute we were waving goodbye to our family at the reception hall, then we were in the air sipping champagne and looking forward to two weeks of fun. A private plane generously provided by one of our guests for a quick getaway.

And then we were in pieces on the ground. Everyone was dead and it was snowing. Everything was on fire, and the fluffy flakes were sizzling as they evaporated in the flames. I moved closer to a burning seat – at least it was warm and my sundress was hardly providing coverage. Jack grabbed our backpacks and said, "We've got to move away from here.

There is fuel everywhere," and "We will stay warm if we start walking," and "is that a dog?" I didn't think moving away from the crash site was a good idea. There was warmth here, and trees to burn. I told Jack I thought it was a man but Jack said, "no, it's a dog." So we followed the dog.

We followed the dog and now I'm alone and scared in the middle of nowhere in a fucking sundress and flip-flops. In the dark. All around me the night is alive with the throbbing chuffs of whatever animals might live in this hell, snapping twigs and the eye watering smell of burning everything. The trees are catching at the tree line and burning leaves are floating like fireflies in the black. And Jack is not here.

This is supposed to be our honeymoon. I'd wanted to spend it in a luxurious hotel, doing nothing but having kinky sex and room service. He'd chosen a nature retreat with only a compass, tents, and what we had in our backpacks. Sex in the woods. In a tent. Not the most romantic man is my Jack. He was insistent, and he won, but after a mind blowing blowjob I extracted a promise of a week away in the location of my dreams. Truly, I didn't care where we went. I only wanted him close to me, skin to skin and revealing in the next step of our lives together. Now he was gone, somewhere. He had been in the lead, his upper body bare and ankle-deep in the white stuff.

He wrapped me in his ugly Hawaiian shirt when I started to shiver. I heard a noise, only a grunt and a shuffle and when I turned back, he'd vanished. It's been hours. I've been wandering in circles for hours since. The flashlight I had secretly packed in my pack is heavy in my hand. Jack will be so angry at me but its weight is a comfort. At least I'd get a few decent blows in before I am ripped apart by some wild thing with teeth, or a pack of drunken hunters out with loaded weapons. And rifles. I'd take the drunks in a heartbeat.

I can't help but laugh and it startles the feathery beasts in the trees, and startles me too. The barely controlled hysterical quality in what should be a joyful noise scares me further and I throttle it back mercilessly. This is not the time to panic, but the beast bites anyway and I run. It is so dark. There isn't even a moon, and the stars are veiled by an overcast sky. I'm screaming in my head – I'm alone on our anniversary in the dark, in the *snow*, afraid, and Jack is *gone, damn him!*

In my panic I catch my toe and feel my shoe tear as I stumble and regain my balance. The momentum carries me on, and I feel a pinch on the back of my neck.

There's no way I've been bitten. It's winter, and there is snow. And a tree, and I can't stop. Another pinch and footsteps crunching behind me. I collapse to my knees just before smashing face first into that trunk.

I can see my breath in the air. It moves like tiny clouds with diamonds in them. There are streaks of blood on the palm of my hand. The footsteps stop directly behind me, and wait. Just wait and every movement is excruciatingly difficult but I try to turn my head. I try to look up and have a small moment of victory as I manage to lift my head before slumping over to my side in the snow. The sun is filtering through the trees and it reminds me of lanterns, and all I can think is, "Oh. It's him."

Follow The Dog: All For Beth

The warm scent of her skin lingers in my nose and lean close to flick my tongue out to taste her. She is as sweet as all my dreams and as intoxicating as beer on a cold night. She was finally mine, finally in my arms.

Her name is Beth, and I've watched her for nearly a year now. Watched her and fell in love with her before I ever even spoken a word to her. She was the one who broke the silence. She's so brave.

The husky sound of her voice when she first said hello is something I will never forget. I spoke to her occasionally after that, leaving small tokens of my devotion on her doorstep, on her desk and then watching her small pleased smile and blush as she spied her presents. I found some bravery, and a few shots of rum.

I awkwardly asked her out the next time I saw her and delighted in her smile when she agreed. It was a fiasco, doomed from the start. I tried to tell her how much I loved her then, and I know it was too soon now, but she'd recoiled and ran out, with not so much as a backwards glance.

I couldn't let her go so I didn't. I watched her smile fade and her eyes turn sad. even my trinkets didn't bring any happiness to her eyes. And then, I watched her meet **him**. Some smarmy son of a bitch that swaggered rather than walked.

His eye followed every single pretty girl like a dog, even going so far once as to grab a blonde's ass while Beth was turned away paying for coffee. The blonde laughed and gave him her number, which he took and stuffed into his jeans. I had him checked out and he was as bad as I thought, worse even, and then she **MARRIED** that jerk. He gets to wake up next to her. He gets to touch her every day. He gets to make her scream. But, she has never smiled at him like she has as my gifts.

The only benefit to this whole mess is that I know that she is the one. He wasn't so self-confident and possessing of male fortitude at the shed. He acted better than me, strutting like a peacock. Then I smashed his knees with the concrete bricks I forced him to haul there.

He laughed at me and told me she would never let me touch her. I smashed his head in with that sledgehammer Daddy left there.

Beth moans in her sleep, throwing her arms over her head and sighing, her bare legs shifting to expose that sweet dark tunnel between her thighs. I can't help myself and touch her, one hand running over her cheek, and the other lightly running up the inside of her inner thigh. Her electricity steals my breath away. So does the way she arches her back when my fingers touch the edge of her warm place. It makes the Bad Thing poke its head up in interest.

Slowly, like a groom would undress his bride, I slide the sharp point of my knife along the buttons of her dress, tilting the blade and flicking the disks off one at a time. They fly a short distance through the air, before landing with a light clatter. The knife cuts through the thin fabric easily and it falls away like silk. Her lovely full breasts are exposed. She is naked underneath, her nipples taut in the coolish air. My hand is still between her legs, and it feels wet down there.

"Why are you doing this?" Her voice makes the Bad Thing twitch in my pants, push against them like it wants out. I don't answer her, and instead lean down and take her nipple between my teeth like that guy did in the movie my sister showed me.

The woman in the movie liked it, and she arched her back the way Beth is doing when my tongue licks the end. I move my fingers over her wet place and push two of my fingers inside her, and do like the movie guy did. My sister said it was a learning video and let me practice after.

Beth tries to close her legs and I bite hard on her nipple and slap her leg hard, then put a third finger in before making my fingers move faster. Her head is shaking back and forth and I think about stopping when she pushes my head down towards where my fingers are. I remember this too.

She makes a funny sound when my tongue touches her there, and pushes my head closer saying *please please make me cum*. I'm not sure where she wants to go but I suck on that little throbbing button and ram my fingers really hard up inside her. My sister said not to stop when she says don't and Beth was yelling it at the top of her lungs.

The Bad Thing hurts now and I want to put it where my fingers are. Beth screams loud and my hand is soaked and so is my chin. It smells like rain and I pull my fingers out and put my tongue inside her, licking all that water away and still it gets wetter. She lifts her head and stares at me with wide eyes, shivering and asking me again why. I stare back, my hand resting on her pleasure center and say "Do you care?" She whines *his* name, *poor Jack*, and now I am angry.

"Jack is dead Beth. D-E-A-D. He isn't coming to save you. He didn't love you like I do. Don't cry. I know you love me too. All my presents." Her jaw drops and I realize she doesn't know. She thought it was him. And he probably took credit for it. I'm glad I bashed his brains in now. I feel her legs trying to close and I push them open, forcing them until her knees touch the bed.

"You think I'm stupid don't you Beth?" I fume while unbuckling my belt and unzipping the stiff zipper of my jeans to let the Bad Thing free. Her eyes get big and she rolls to the side of the bed, and jumps to her feet. I am between her and the door and she sees her mistake – wrong side my love. The Bad Thing is pulsing in my hand and I smile as I walk towards the woman of my dreams, ready to consummate the marriage that should be ours.

Follow The Dog: Sterling's Demise

The bed is so soft and the room warm. I stretch and smile, thinking I' won after all and Jack had flown us somewhere romantic for our honeymoon instead of some stupid nature retreat or whatever. I knew he was hiding something. My body isn't responding when I try to move, or is slow to do so and I don't mind. The last few days have been exhausting. I'm just tired and his fingers running along the contours of my cheek while the others softly caress the inside of my thigh feels too good to fight. Jack's fingers linger dangerously close to my sweet spot, and I arch against it. He'd insisted we wait until we were on our honeymoon and I was tired of waiting.

He's playing dangerous, my new husband, and moves his hand from my cheek and not my thigh.

My eyes won't open but try harder when the light ping of things landing on the floor catches my attention. The buttons on my sundress. It was new! He threatened to tear them off. Then an odder sound, not of fabric tearing but close enough and I feel the cool air creep along my skin. Marriage has kicked up his libido and I'm not at all unhappy about it. The thought of him finally using his imagination excited me immensely, and the easy slide of his fingertips closer to where I wanted them the most made me wetter. I could feel his eyes on me, visually licking like a tongue across my hard nipples, making me hotter. The anticipation was excruciating.

"Why are you doing this," I moan, delighted when Jack bites my nipple and licks the end, feeling the sensation like a direct wire to desire and finally he puts two fingers inside me, then three. It feels so good, every nerve ending alive. My arms move – they move and I use them to push his head down, needing to feel his mouth on my clit and begging him to let make me cum before I implode. He obliges, lighting my body on fire until I soak his finger and nearly drown him when I explode, screaming his name and then again as his fingers pull out of me and his long strong tongue goes in. Sex has never been this way with Jack.

I lift my head, with my fingers still wrapped in his hair to stare into the eyes of my husband and see a familiar face staring at me, and one that didn't belong there. I shiver, and his fingers twitch inside me, pressing against the sensitive walls and making my pussy quiver. I ask him why, how, where is Jack and his free hand presses hard on my clit, before he snaps, "Why? Do you care?" Of course I care, and he snarls, "Jack is dead Beth. D-E-A-D. He isn't coming to save you. He didn't love you like I do. Don't cry. I know you love me too. All my presents"

Sterling Crim. He killed Jack. He had his mouth on me and finger fucked me and killed my husband over the fact I walked out on him on the one and only date we ever had.

No, those gifts were from Jack. I try to close my legs and pull away, and Sterling slaps the tender skin on my thighs hard, and pushes them to the bed so that my sex is open and exposed to his eyes. I am afraid and he is angry, asking if I think he is stupid while he unbuckles his pants and I see his erection. He was larger than Jack and for a moment I stared before rolling to my side and falling off of the bed. As soon as I get to my feet I see my mistake and know I am trapped. Wrong side stupid. No one is coming, he is right, so I have to save myself.

"Let's start over Beth. What do you say," he says quietly as he comes towards me, his hard dick in hand and licking his lips, "It is our wedding night after all?"

Deranged and dangerous. He planned this, the sick fuck, down to getting an invitation to our wedding. and now he wants to take Jack's place. He wants to fuck me and pretend that he is the one when he killed the man I chose to be, and I cringe when he kisses my collarbone hard enough to fall backwards on to the bed.

Sterling wastes no time, and shoves my legs back before burying himself to the hilt, and pounding into me like a man who has never had sex before. I see Jack in the doorway, his temple bleeding and lips swollen and I start to cry, ashamed. He shakes his head with a smile and I understand immediately and writhe under Sterling, gasping.

Sterling redoubles his efforts, each thrust making the air in my lungs huff out and scream for him to fuck me harder as Jack whispers in my ear, telling me to cum and I do, soaking the sheets under me and making Sterling pull back violently. I call him back, letting his eyes wander over my wide open legs and the pleasure palace between, and offer to blow his mind. He seems torn and cautiously comes closer, undecided as to whether to continue as before or let me touch him. "It's not like the movie," he mutters.

I take the choice out of his hands and wrap my lips around the bulbous head of his cock, sucking it deep into my throat and letting the tip of my tongue dance along the shaft. I can taste myself on him and suck harder, knowing his inexperience would make him shoot his wad before long and clutch his ballsack in my hand, wanting to make him nervous. Sterling groans and grabs handfuls of my hair in his fists to fuck my mouth like he did my pussy.

Jack grins from the chair in the corner, and I dig my nails into the soft flesh of Sterling's sac and pull down hard, choking as he cums and it sprays the back of my throat while he screams. He won't let go and I pull harder, hearing the skin rip and the hot gush of blood that follows. He is jittering and holding my head tight to his crotch, jittering while I twist the meat of his sex in my fist and ram the nails of my other into the soft muscle of his thigh.

Finally, he lets go and I fall away, my hand covered in blood and gore and he lays panting with his ruined crotch glimmering in the overhead bulb. "I loved you Beth. I'll die without you," Sterling wheezes, holding his hand out to me.

"So die," I offer, turning to wash the blood from myself at the kitchen sink. I can hear him trying to move behind me and glance at his struggle before raiding the small closet for clothes and footwear. Jack stands by the window, his eyes full of mist, staring at the sun.

My first morning as a widow dawns bright and full of hope, my new life over before it had a chance to begin, and I step out the front door to a dooryard full of rescue. Jack strokes my cheek and kisses my forehead, the chill of his lips fading as the first officer speaks to me.

14

Bacillius Blue

Some monsters are hatched out of the subconscious of a few whack jobs that seek reassurance in torturing millions with their sick and depraved imaginings, and Ella Buck gives thanks every day these for said sickos and their predispositions towards probing and fucking around with the fear factor. If not for these few Physicians of Phantasy, humanity would not have the delightfully inhuman monsters that we do and thus our imaginations would be sadly lacking. Lacking in the reality that really sticks in the hippocampus and preys there like a particularly venomous and beautiful spider. She forgot that some monsters are made, some out their own contrivance and some by no fault of their own, and she was sad to learn that she fell into the latter category.

Ella was on the edge of thirty and far too jaded towards humans as a species to consider any long-term exposure to them as a whole. She had no fear of being alone and wasn't really, if you counted her five roommates and she did. Though one, if she were honest with herself, she would gladly throw herself in front of a train if he would just fucking talk to her instead of watching her every move - instead of brushing against her when he passes.

She knows there is something, some kind of connection because he returns to place his eye to the crack in her door every damned night while she undresses and pulls his pud while she does a little striptease for him or lies on the bed and gets herself off while watching him jack off in the mirror. Sed. God Sed. She loves Sed and will gladly admit if anyone ever asked, but he never has and nor has anyone else. She thought she was quite obvious.

He had been odd at dinner, unusually quiet and sullen instead of the animated chatter and gestures that kept them all laughing. Instead he used his fork to push the food around and then finally pushed it away without taking a bite. Not a word he spoke during that meal, but the few times she chanced a fleeting look, it was met with direct eye contact.

Ella was sure he was going to finally do something about it and tonight there had been a bottle of exquisite 2007 Finca Bella Vista at dinner and too many long looks across the table.

An extra joint mixed heavenly with the coffee and vanilla aftertaste and had left her inhibitions running amok instead of carefully locked away.

She'd known Sed would be there shortly and left the door open while she took a quick shower. The door was ajar sufficiently that she hoped as she towel dried her hair, that it would entice him to come into the bedroom and finally show her that he wanted her. She was hardly making it difficult for him. He didn't fail to prove her right. Sed stood there in the doorway watching her flick her clit with the freshly manicured tips of one hand while her other slowly and with deliberation fucked herself with the new dildo she had bought yesterday. He let his dick free from his jeans, and fixedly watched her pant and wriggle on the bed and was silent while he openly stroked himself in full view of anyone passing by.

Too much longer and she would have begged him to ride her like a stolen bike, but tonight there was no coaxing or demands necessary. Sed had crept up on her while her eyes were closed in ecstasy and yanked the rubber tool from her hand with an expression that was both hungry and aroused.

Ella moaned in relief when he buried himself to the hilt and his balls slapped against her ass. The relief didn't last long and she saw now that Sed was not himself. He was like rock and larger than she first anticipated, far larger than what she had glimpsed in the mirror and his thrusts were hard enough hurt. It was still far more pleasure than she'd ever experienced and

She dug her nails into his back groaning his name. Sed didn't hold back, not even when she began slapping at his chest and calling his name. All she could do was spread her legs further when his lunges began to make her insides ache and she came with a sharp cry when he nuzzled into her full breast and bit deeply into the soft tissue. She had wanted him in every way including this but now she was numb she couldn't feel herself cum anymore. It seemed like hours that he been pounded her pussy and every time her body spasmed, Sed's tongue would probe into the wound on her tit. It was a never-ending cycle of agony and pleasure, and she was lost in it.

His movements changed again, more mechanical and increasingly vicious. Ella tried to speak his name and began to cry when his cock kept battering her walls. She kept losing her breath.

This time she did scream when she came and Sed snapped out of the robotic loop he had been trapped in; he became a rabid dog, shaking his head and snarling words she didn't understand and covering her face with the thick ropy strands of drool that were hanging from her mouth. Her elbows locked as she pushed back against him, sobbing with the painful thrusts he was still punishing her with.

He balled his fists and started hitting her with every other pump of his hips, alternating with bite of his teeth. Ella wore marks all over her face and chest, from his teeth and hands and he just wouldn't stop, even holding her legs apart and down so that she couldn't buck up or move away. The pain wasn't pleasure anymore – it was agony that stole her breath when she came again out of self-defense. Her hand fell back and she felt the smooth ceramic of her bedside table. She had been cleaning and unplugged it earlier today and now she tightened her fingers around it, shouting his name once more, then smashed him in the temple with the lamp with everything she had. The black holes that were his eyes met hers in momentary surprise and he twisted her nipple ferociously and ejaculated before he gurgled and blacked out, landing hard on top of her.

She had sobbed for a few minutes and then with her shaky arms and legs managed to push his dead weight off of her and scramble naked for the door, pausing to lock the handle before slamming it behind her and sliding down to the floor in tears. Ella gathered herself together and sighed harshly when she finally managed to get to her feet. The flesh between her thighs was throbbing and it felt wet and hot with every step she took towards the bathroom and the water she wished would wash it all away.

The human condition is that we should all die and be resurrected by the immunity the antibiotics we continually ingest affords us. Though that is not exactly the way Ella wants to spend forever. She'd rather have spent eternity with Sedrick but he is likely unconscious, dead or awake and pissed to beat hell.

The air is over-warm and she shivers in the molten tub of water like an abandoned child, sobbing deep in her chest from the ache in her center that just won't subside. The water comforts her like a warm embrace and she lifts a shaky hand to brush the damp curls from her face with her eyes on the door.

Downstairs she can hear only the mutterings of several people in discussion, the remnants of a holiday dinner gone awry and she hopes that everyone will escape untouched, but knows it's not even a remote possibility. Her roommates are hardly the type to be quiet let alone give privacy.

Human contact is not something Ella wants at the moment, in fact, it repulses her so much that she's already decided not to have her wounds treated much less seen by anyone but herself. It doesn't matter now that she is dead. There was one less thing to concern her raving mind.

She still breathes, though it hurt her body to do so, and she weeps in the heat with her hands clamped over her tender mouth lest someone hear and come investigate. She breathes and her heart still beats and her eyes still leak but she could feel it working in her veins, devouring every healthy cell in its path on its race to her brain. And it was cold. There was no way to stop it, not really other than killing herself and certainly much too late now. By the time she works up the nerve to blow her own head off it will all be a moot point; it is much too late for her and God help her, for the five other people who reside with her.

The water is an ugly pinkish color, so much more diluted than what he brought to the surface of her skin with his teeth and his fingernails. With his fists. Ella wonders if he is still in there, waiting for her and hunches over her knees in denial. A low moan escapes her mouth and she presses her hands tighter to her swollen lips. She doesn't want to die, not yet and her eye catches Sed's silver straight razor in the corner and she stiffens in the cooling water.

It's getting more difficult to choke back the screams that keep threatening to burst out of her mouth. Every fiber of her being is singing scream and she is locked up by her own awareness. Sed's razor is in her hand now and she flips it open to expose it's incredibly sharp edge.

He sharpens it every morning after using it on his stubbly face. It would split her skin deeply and this would all be over in no time.

Ella didn't want to hurt him and she is afraid of what he has given her and of what happens now. The unknown is more terrifying to her than anything else in the world. The water is cold and she lurches from the tub to pant and stare at the door. Sed. Jesus she had to get to Sed before it was too late to tell him. Pausing to wrap a towel around her tall, well-developed frame, she steps out into the hallway and heads down to her bedroom.

The door is still closed and she takes that as a bad omen. Sedrick was a kind and loving man, but she had seen the evidence of his temper on the walls in the garage. He would be livid by now, were he conscious. It hurts between her legs, every movement her cunny twinge both in hunger and in pain, and she wouldn't change it. The pain keeps her alert and alive.

Sed's hand is protruding from behind her bed. That is not where she left him and there wasn't that much blood before. It stains the carpet and the bed is smeared with streaks of crimson and littered with the broken remains of the lamp she smashed into his temple before running for her life. Sed's hand doesn't move and Ella's fear that there is now a dead body where the man she loves used to be makes her sick to her stomach. She lets out the breath that she hadn't known she was holding out in a rush when the fingers twitch. The next inhale sets her nerves on edge and makes the hair on her neck stand straight up.

Humans are born with the innate knowledge of hunting and know instinctively the scent of blood in the air. It's one of those unheard of facts but still Ella knows that smell like she does the familiar scent of Sed's aftershave or the smell of rain in the air. It's more than blood and there is a lot of it. The hand twitches again in a jerky motion, the curled index finger relaxes and seems point her away but terror in her throat is also paralyzing her legs.

There is a wet squelchy sound from the other side of the bed. It reminds her of the time they were camping in the foothills and she stepped in the rotting remains of a ground squirrel, that same watery splat. The hand is twitching consistently now and the wet sounds are accompanied by soft grunts and exhales.

Jesus what the hell is going on here, she thinks to herself, taking two delicate and nervous steps forward.

Just below the edge of the bed is a mop of curly blond hair that shivers on the head it is attached to. That head bobs down and she loses sight of it, thankfully while her mind processes what she has just witnessed. Not Sed on the floor but Sed kneeling at the knees of someone else. Grunting, wet sounds – was he blowing someone in her room for fuck sake? The mouth sized wound on her breast is burning like a motherfucker and it is turning a deeper red at the edges.

Goddamn him for giving her some infection. She just wanted him to fuck her, not make her sick. Rage that she hadn't felt in such a long time is now an overflowing mess that was about to explode. Sweating lightly, Ella takes a deep breath and was about to snarl Sed's name when his head came back up and she freezes instead, the breath trapped in her lungs.

She can just see Sed's eyes, and they are rolled up in some kind of gastronomic ecstasy as he chews; he moans in an erotic manner before diving back down and she moves quickly to the edge of the bed and drops to her knees. Grant. Sweet Jesus, those gorgeous full lips of his are gone and so is his nose;

Ella glances down Grant's long body to where Sed is hairline deep in Grant's guts, with his fingers hooked into the edge of the open hole like some kind of ravenous beast. Ella's tit is on fire and her fingers come away bloody when she wipes away the quiet grief that is eating at her.

The skin under her eyes comes away and burns her hands, making her wipe them on the towel she still wore. Shit, what the fuck is moving so quickly inside her?

She can hear the others in the kitchen in raised voices and making loud lewd comments about Grant and Sedrik and naturally including her. The desire to rip them apart was strong enough to make her growl and stare longingly at the door. Sed looks up at her with his face coated in gore and tissue with a feral growl when she makes the hungry sound, and pushes himself to his feet in a smooth motion. He wipes his clawed hand across his lips, tearing small pieces of his flesh away with the blood that covers them.

He starts babbling nonsensical gibberish that stuns her and awakens some deep-seated fury in her chest. Ella stands as well, trembling in a feverish sweat with a sneer. This asshole is snarling at *her* after he did *this?!* Every night he stands with his eye to the god damned crack in the fucking door and when he finally finds the backbone and balls to fuck her, he infects her with someth-   *Bacillus Blue*

The flashes of memory that flash in her mind are painful, agonizing to the point her body contorts and she howls. Sedrick is crouching like an animal ready to defend his meal and she when the spasm eases, Ella responds in kind, curling her lip up to its pink under flesh like a predatory cat. She is losing her battle with the parasite in her body, it seems easier to let it win even when he darts forward and breathes corruption heavily into her face. There is no need for a lamp this time. Ella is stronger frightened even as her humanity ebbs away than he is lost in whatever insanity has turned his brain to soup.

With a swift swipe, she tears his throat out with a yawp and laughs as she is bathed in his blood. It is almost boiling and he stands with his black eyes wide and snapping at her face with his strong white teeth. A savage swipe of his hand tears the towel from her body and she feels the slick liquid slide over her bare breasts.

"Goodbye Sedrick. I love you," she rumbles, collapsing to the floor, once again trapped under his dead weight, but this time she is able to toss his ruined and boneless shell away with little effort. There are footsteps in the foyer, and the high-pitched voices of the truly frightened waft up the stairs to my ears.

Downstairs are three healthy bodies that would stay sturdy while they continued to pass on whatever this is and she intended to make them suffer as she is. Ten steps to the crest of the stairs. Eighteen to the main level and the fresh meat. The coldness has turned her mind into desolate place and she relishes the way her bare feet leave perfect prints on the creamy carpet. The way her friends and roomies call out to her as she descends, and then, like deer in the headlights, freeze when they see the infection in her eyes.

They fall easily enough; Aubrey doesn't even attempt to make a break for it and only closes her eyes when Ella kisses her on her soft lips and tweaks her nipple. Breaking the kiss, Ella leans down to nip at the place where Aubrey's shoulder and neck meet then punches her fist through her middle. Ria screams long and loud and bolts for the front door. She forgot that she triple locks it every time she comes in. Catching her low, she hits the ground with a huff and a whimper when Ella's teeth puncture the meat at her hip and her hand slips up under the short skirt Ria perpetually wears. Ella's fingers find her bare beneath and she dips two digits as far inside Ria's snug hole while she buries her face in her warm fragrant flesh and commenced ripping her stomach apart. The bitch dies as she soaks Ella's hand with her juices.

Only Piper remains. She grabs the baseball bat from the umbrella stand and Ella hears a familiar voice from the Livingroom. Someone had the TV on and they were reporting incidences of violence all over the city, with many deaths and hospitals filled to capacity. "Bacillus Blue has officially arrived. We urge you to stay home and take plenty of rest and fluids," were the last words Ella hears. Piper's sweater had slipped off her shoulder and she bore a mouth shaped wound much like own and she laughs when Piper roars at her, swinging the bat to kill, and cocking her head when the bat claps into Ella's hand with a heathy smack and no flinch. Outside, sounds of death and destruction call, and the lone shriek of a woman turned beast. Piper is shouting nonsense words and drooling, gesturing towards the door and smiling malevolently when Ella licks her teeth and shrugs.

Outside the sun is setting. Piper grabs Ella's hand and grins into her cruor covered face with a sort of glee. The last vestiges of sanity were lost as humanity rattles its last breath. Across the nation, society has broken down, and the public has become a lunatic mass. On the television screen in Ella's living room, the image rolls, showing a photo from New York City. Someone had used black spray-paint to scrawl three words on the sidewalk and they were partially obscured by a pool of blood.

Beware Bacillus Blue

15

Thicker Than Water

The sign on the door swings back and forth in the air-conditioned lobby; the arc of its enthusiastic movement slows even as I thumb the lock and stand a moment in the light of the blazing sun to watch the small gathering crowd in the parking lot. Word travels fast in a small town and this time was no exception. I wonder idly how that could be when no one here has had use of any device to do as much as text.

I slide the flat of my palm along my right hip, smoothing the self-conscious wrinkles that my hand is sure were there. A thirty-pound weight loss in recent months has left my confidence sobbing on the floor, where I would rather be myself. Lying on the floor and pretending to be dead was not going to get me where I needed to be, and so I stay on my feet and observe.

A bunch of trained monkeys I can't help but think, amused. The awkward wiggle-walk of an oh-so-mature teenage girl with rather large breasts and a vacant, come-hither stare catches my eye. Several lean suited men sipping coffee ogle her nubile curves like hyenas, each flashing her an encouraging predatory grin. She leans against the front panel of my cherry red 'Cuda and the sight of the keys hanging from her belt loops scraping against the paint makes me want to rip the little bitch's throat out. Soon enough and if I was lucky, I would obliterate the little snatch and teach her a lesson about respect.

Someone thumps in the quiet and the noise startles me back from my murderous plotting. Behind me, a small silent crowd rustles like blackbirds, waiting. The air feels thin as my hand becomes sweat-slick and the gun I had stolen begins to slip. I have no choice but to transfer it to my other hand, and wipe my left palm lightly down the length of my thigh. The pistol has heft and smells strongly of oil and testosterone. Of course it would, in light of who I had taken it from. He wouldn't need it where he was going, and I was in need of a working weapon now. I hope I killed the motherfucker but a quick glance tells me that he should be regaining consciousness soon.

The old woman's whine is making me antsy and the sound of her labored breathing seems to be purposefully irritating. I turn on my heel with a grace that shocks even me to stare down at her, secretly relishing the way she recoils with a wide-eyed terror that probably should upset me. It doesn't though. I haven't directly threatened anyone, yet, the gun in my hand I'd only vaguely waved in a menacing direction and they dropped to the floor like stones. Actions do indeed speak louder. These assholes have never listened to a word that I have uttered even once in their poor excuses for lives, and I've known them for all of mine. Such is the way of the privileged. They don't know what it means to suffer for anything.

That childlike anxiety the old cow's eyes makes me feel a little bit bad for her, for them; after all, I was apparently in polite, civilized society and it's hardly social convention to wave a loaded weapon at a bank full of the community's finest. That niggling humanity is nothing more than a fleeting fancy and is thankfully gone in a blink. Not one of the individuals in this room has ever given a tin shit about me when they were destroying my world, why should I care if I destroy theirs? I'm not a terrible person but I can't care anymore, not until I have the confirmation I've nearly killed myself to get.

The sun is brutal even for July and it burns the back of my neck through the untreated windows. Taking in the faces of my unfortunate captives, I straighten my spine and consider my next move. Each is a face I know as well as my own reflection, and behind their frightened expressions lies a slyer, knowing smirk. They know why they are here and think they are smarter than I am, with their noses in the air and the lazy savoir faire of the nouveau riche, they smirk amongst themselves and I am suddenly inspired by the terrified masks they wear.

"What are you going to do to us!?" the querulous voice of the old woman rings out and echoes between the silences and shouts of the Hewe Police Force. A glance over my shoulder reveals them bumbling about in the crowded parking; while several of them stand, watching me watching them with their hands on the butts of their pistols.

Surely, were I a man, I would be dead by now but put the criminal in a dress that shows a little leg and some cleavage, they turn into teenage horn dogs without a brain to share. To my left more proof of their witlessness; two of the town's finest in blue bang off each other and fall on their asses in an improvisational slapstick kind of way. I can't help but giggle.

"Are you *laughing*? Waving a loaded gun in the faces of the town council is amusing to you?!" God I hate that woman. Tiffani Kartish, the pretty young matron around town, formerly Tiffani Howard, the Mayor's daughter, was once the biggest whore at

Richter High. According to the little blue book that I found in the bathroom one afternoon, she'd been down on every member of both football teams, the AV club and at least half of the teachers including the ultra-conservative Miss Clark. If I was to believe the book I still had and the notes there, combined with the fearful expression on Tiffani's face, I'll bet she walked weird for at least a week. Frigid my ass. I'm saving Tiff for last, and the whole town will hear her scream for mercy before I'm through.

"Well? Answer her Junie!" the old crone demands again in that snooty nasal whine I fucking despise, "What are you going to do to us!?" She thinks she is better than I, better than anyone she views as less than she is, when her own soul is hardly lily white. Showing off again would get her killed and allowing her to get away with it would set a poor example. I consider killing her as sort of an object lesson to the rest and entertain the thought more seriously as the hag grows more agitated. Her son

Victor places his hand on her injured cheek and glares out the window at the sun that was beginning to descend in the sky. The born again virgin, realizing she has support, adds a strident whine to her complaints. Some things never change.

I fire a shot at the old woman that goes purposefully wide, and smile as a chip of the custom marble tile closest to her right elbow flies up and slices her cheek open. The collar of the high-necked white blouse she wears turns a bright red in no time and it nearly glows in the natural light. With her thin lips forming a perfect O that accentuates her wrinkles, she lifts her hand to her cheek, where her fingers trace the lips of the wound that gapes like a small mouth.

"I haven't decided Olivia, but perhaps, you could shut your pie hole while I think. Stop looking so shocked, after all, this is partly your fault." Her mouth trembles, closes, then opens again like a landlocked fish and her hands shake as tears fall from her rheumy eyes. "I tried not to hate you, any of you. So much effort to play nice when all this time you were playing a game that you thought only *you* could win. Letting the hatred for you, all of you feels so much better than pretending," I say to no one in particular and to each them, all spoken in a thoughtful conversational tone without raising my voice an octave.

The tip of the gun is still warm and I kneel to press it up hard under Olivia Kartish's chin, "Keep. Your. Mouth. Shut. Or the next time you open it will be your last. Give me a thumbs up if you understand." She gives an enthusiastic response and I smack her with the butt of the gun in the left temple to the angry shouts of her husband. At least she will be quiet for a while. I need to consider a few other things before the fun begins.

They clamor around her as I consider my choices. They are few, but at least I have choices. As I see the situation, there are only a few avenues open to me at this stage. I could take my pound of flesh, kill myself and let them believe they survived me. I could kill them all, which is my preference, or I could force the cops to do it. No matter what I decide, I am a walking corpse who has yet begun to rot and nothing else matters but that confirmation of death. Sick of the scene in front of me, I turn away, brushing my hair from my eyes to scan the crowd for the cunt that scratched my car. I still owe her a lesson.

Twin holes burn in my head, full of heavy disapproval that weights the stare. I can deal with that, after all, taking shots at old women is hardly something that society finds acceptable. What is uncomfortable, however, is the awareness of eyes like fingers stripping away my clothing and the excruciating sensation my flesh being peeled away; first lustfully then with growing vicious intent. "Stop eyeballing me Timmy. I hate it."

The knowing chuckle that has always made me crazy rolls through the place, lightly mocking as I curse inside and cock the gun. I'll blow his fucking head off for being a dicksickle but I was so sure the bastard was still unconscious. I need to pay better attention. "What are you going to do about it? Take another shitty shot at Mom? Kill me? Fuck me? You know you want to. You never could resist the way I..." Tiffani interrupts, gasping and I fight the urge to blow her damned stupid head off. She needs to be last.

Oh but that smug son of a bitch. I want to cut his throat now just to end the self-confident show but then realize he is much more useful to me in another capacity. It didn't mean he couldn't learn a lesson, however. "Shut it. You're right - I never could resist and neither could you. She was never going to be enough for you, everyone could see it. But hey, you aren't in charge here. I am. The next outburst and she gets a prize." Watching Tiffani's round brown eyes bulge unattractively in their sockets when the barrel of the gun settles in her direction is such a delight.

Timmy chuckles again and I can feel his rapt attention like a tongue on my thighs and in between. It pisses me off and I let out a frustrated groan.

"I warned you. Dammit Timmy, you never fucking listen to me." For fuck sake – The right side of Tiffani's head explodes in a spray of shredded brain tissue, blood and bone that covers the horrified screaming faces of those closest to her. Her body jitters uncontrollably with her heels slapping in rapid tempo on the floor then relaxes along with her sphincter and bladder.

Her blood is much darker than I expected it to be. Thicker too. What little mind she possessed is now a mess on the floor. "Any more questions?"

The shrill ringing of the telephone shatters what little peace I'd gained since this all began, and I was glad for the distraction from the vomiting noises and the hum of the air conditioner. Naturally, it would be the Chief of Police, that fucking moron. "Someone pick that up and watch what you say." Timmy slowly rises to his feet and reaches over the counter with his eyes on mine. Clearing his throat, he barks, "Yes?" into the receiver. I can hear the frantic questions that the Chief is asking and although I can't hear actual words, the tone conveys enough.

"Mrs. T. Kartish. Yes. Yes, I'm sure! Her head is all over the fucking floor. Is that sure enough for you?" Timmy's voice cracks slightly and I would swear on a stack of Stephen King novels that I hear humor, though the down-turned corners of his full lips tell a different story.

"Mrs. Oliva Kartish has a cut cheek and is unconscious. No, she's not injured badly." He listens a moment and blinks out the window in disbelief, then around at the four remaining captives.

"Absolutely not! Chief Sawton, have you lost your mind?"

I grab the phone and point to the floor with the barrel of the gun. Timmy drops without giving me a second look. Good. The Chief is yelling in frustration about his plan and I slam it down hard enough to make the desk shiver. "Junie." I don't want to hear another word and observe two of the chief's boys in blue right outside the doors. "It's not enough for you that you stole everything from me is it?" His head is shaking slowly back and forth and his spoiled Ivy League younger brother, Victor, laughs in a low voice while gesturing at the cop to the left of the door with a knowing expression. "Say goodbye to your brother Timmy." Victor stops laughing immediately and shrugs his shoulders.

"Junie *no*!" The top of Victor's head flies apart, much like his sister-in-law's had, but the bullet doesn't take him low enough and he is still laughing; now standing, Victor shuffles his feet and he spins around and around with the blood trickling over the edge of his shattered skull. He is dancing like a demented doll and singing while his father cries.

"Jesus Junie," Timmy whispers sickly from the floor beside me, "just. Just end it okay? Junie, please." I can hear the tears in his voice and watch nauseated when Victor turns to me and points with a shaky finger.

"Ohhhh *Juuuuuunnnnniiiieeee…*" Victor sings in a garbled sing-song voice, his eyeballs bulging when his hands flutter like birds to sink into his brain. He screams as he begins pulling handfuls of the grey-pink tissue from the ruined shell of his mind. "YOU DID THIS TO ME! ASSBAG! CUMDUMPSTER! YOOOOOOOOOOOOOU DID IT."

I can't stand to listen to his filthy mouth any longer and fire a bullet into his right eye that ends his shitty singing. The officers have dropped their weapons in shock and I take the opportunity to end them as well. Two shots, two hats fly in the air and twin geysers of scarlet stain the sidewalk.

"You, Pops, get your scrawny ass up off that floor, pick up that phone and call the Sawton. If that," and here I stab him with my glare and gesture with the barrel of my own weapon towards the shattered windows, "happens again, I will cut off every one of your fingers and your tongue and shove it up your daughter-in-law's snatch. They were up there often enough; it should feel like home.

"Make sure the Chief understands that all of your deaths will be on his head. *I will kill your wife and your son.* I will cut you apart and then let you live. Do you understand me?"

The old man's hand slips in blood trying to stand and he lands face first on the expensive marble that has caused more than one injury in this place. He lays there sobbing for a moment and then pushes himself up to his knees, using Tiffani's body as leverage. The old fuck squeaks when he realizes and wipes his sodden palm on his fine silk trousers before finally getting his ass off the floor. "I asked you if you understood."

He freezes and then nods without a word, familiarly typing the code that will allow him access to the phone and the cash drawers with no shake in his fingers whatsoever. "Pops." I hear my own voice loud in my ears and watch him shudder but never break stride. "I know what you've been doing. One fuck up and I will make sure that children scream when they see you on the street, and that women vomit." Timmy's hand finds my ankle and I look down into his miserable face. I want to feel something. I really do want to feel anything but I can't. I have nothing left to give.

"June. Please." Pretty words won't change a thing, not now. Before he abandoned me, I might have never been here. I might have left off and let this go. But that was then. His hand drops away and I lash out to kick him twice in the gut with the pointed toe of my shoe. "I have felt *that* every day for the past three months. Hurts, doesn't it?"

I had been only half listening to the patriarch when his holier-than-thou attitude kicks in and then the old pervert has my full attention. "Just shoot her Orval. Two of your idiots are dead because you won't do what you've committed to do. Pull the fucking trigger or you might as well blow your own head off. You'll wish you did." The front window is gone and shards of broken glass soar through the lobby like bullets. Timmy has me on the ground, covering my body with his weight and taking the sharpest spray to save my hide.

"Get away from me," I rasp into his face, and shove him away, "your father wants me dead. He planned this as much as I did Timmy, and then he slowly took everything from me. You. Let. Him... so get the fuck off of me!" This time I pistol whip him and scramble away before he can trap me again. Motherfucker has a hard head.

"Hey Pops!" The old bastard makes his first mistake and lets me know exactly where he is. The second mistake was losing his nerve and bolting from relative safety. I cut his ass down with a bullet to the leg and watch him skid and curl up on the floor. He moans and screams like a rich girl forced to clean toilets.

"Coming Pops. Just hang tight daddy-o. I have this one small thing -" I sing and crouch beside Timmy to smile into his starry-eyed expression. I may have hit him too hard.

"I could have left when you did, you know, I wanted to but they," I gesture behind me with the pistol and genuinely smile when the crone cries out, "convinced me to stay. Your daddy was the one who introduced me to Asher. He was also the one who killed him, in that office right back there. Blew his brains out all over the wall while our daughter watched in her stroller, but you know that, so don't look at me like I don't have reason."

Patriarch Pete is still whining. Jesus he bitches hard. He isn't really hurt bad enough to die, although if he doesn't quit the howling I might blow his face off just to get a moment's peace. His wife has joined him and has her hand over his mouth in an attempt to stop the braying.

"Shut up Peter. She's coming," the hag says in a dead voice and I feel that righteous swelling in my chest. His blathering stops and his head falls to the side as I approach.

"June. Please, you don't understand – "

"Save it Pops. *You* don't understand -you may live in a small town but your ethics are big city. I know everything, Daddy-O. Your employer, Frederick Elias, was very forthcoming with information Pete. It is truly amazing what a little incentive can bring. You are an extremely naughty boy. Judging from the horrified expression, I suspect that it's time to have a chat with Olivia here."

The shock that crosses her face would be hilarious, if it weren't so pitiful, and she looks past me to where her son lays quietly, then into the face of her husband. Outside the shattered windows I can hear the chief yelling at his minions to keep it down and then continues yelling his plans. This place is a fucking zoo and I have things to do before I walk out of here. "If you try to run, any of you, I will kill you, no matter where you run to. Behave yourselves and I may just let you go." I have no intentions of letting any of them live but it is enough to give them hope, and I see it in their eyes.

Pops has graciously left the gate open, done so unconsciously when he flew from safety and it saves me from having to force the code from him. I'm tired now and out of habit, snag my purse from the counter where I had left it. Pops had shown me a secret cache of cash and other valuables a few years ago, things that he had then claimed not even his wife was aware of. I have no doubt that Timmy is fully aware and that Victor knew too before his mind became spray.

Behind me the air conditioning thumps and a fresh breeze of cool air travels across my bare legs that makes me shiver. I blink and shake my head to clear it. This was no time to daydream. I had to get back to business. I still had three to kill here and then the added bonus of the coppers outside, all still immersed in a giant circle jerk just outside the building.

The desk is an old relic from somewhere or another. Pops told me that too when he showed me his treasure trove and told me a few truths about what my life would entail should I marry his son. Ingenious design, it truly is, some engineer's brainchild I suppose, and the poor thing ended up here in the Kartish whorehouse.

I can't help myself and crouch down to run my finger along the barely perceptible line that matches the grain of the wood. Just one more move and I can finish here, and live out the rest of my life in comfort. Using the desk edge for leverage, I move quietly to my feet and around the side towards the last thing in my way.

Timmy grabs me in the darkened office, pushing me forward until my face is pressed against the wall and he breathes laughter in my ear before spinning me around. I can feel him hard against my belly, his hot and insistent erection letting me know exactly what was in store. There is no way in hell I was going to let him fuck me. Not in here, not now. Once upon a time I would already be assuming his favorite position but now. No. Oh but his hands feel good, the way they travel everywhere, warm on my ass and the way they pull my dress up to my hips. "Nothing has changed," he growls into my ear after finding me bare.

True to form and with no preamble, his fingers slide roughly into my body. No nothing has changed and he shamelessly brings me quickly to orgasm.

"You never could resist."

I never could resist. I could swear he was a demon; the way I was trapped from the first smile. I never could resist the way he took me over, not the way his fingers fuck me until my knees give out, or the way he tongues circles my clit like some slippery starving creature. With that combined sensation, no girl stood a chance, least of all me. I nearly drown him in my pleasure and he chuckles again, that same smug, annoying laugh that still makes me want to bash his fucking head in. Or I would have had he not effectively, quite cleverly, disarmed me.

His beast has been released and the soft tip teases along my slit, searching for entry and I dart forward to whisper in his ear. I am quite clever too. Yes, admittedly, I want it as much has he very clearly does and woman is not meant to live without intercourse, sexual or otherwise, and still I despise that I am still so weak. It doesn't matter when he carries my weight easily to his father's desk and slides his blade deep into my sheath as I am set down.

"Like the first time Junie. Remember?" He huffs into my face with each thrust and I nod, riding the desire train while I plot his end. It feels like he was slamming his entire weight into my cunny and I just can't help myself. God help me, I fuck him back with all my strength, and lacerate his back with my nails when I cum.

"Just like old times," I snarl back, digging deeper and enjoying the surprised displeasure that colors his eyes. He hated it then too and predictably he increases his tempo, ready to drop his seed once again and that is something that I have no intentions of letting happen.

"Where is my daughter, Timmy?" I whisper in his ear and laugh when he freezes in mid-thrust and his proud member trembles then wilts inside me. So he does know. Admittedly, this whole scenario was premeditated, down to the sun soaked parking spot and this little interlude. The fact was that it was he that could never resist, and I've spent three months plotting and searching for my little girl. I even bought a little house under an assumed name, in a quiet place.

I did try to play ball, I did my best to play the game and still it wasn't enough. Now he is staring at me in horror and backs away with his spent member flopping gamely. I do feel bad, but I can't take it back and I won't stop now. "Timmy. Where is my daughter?" I'm sitting on his father's desk with my legs spread and he is just standing there staring at me like I am some undefined animal. I know she is dead, in my heart I know it but I need to hear the words and I will hear them one way or another, either from his lips or his parents.

I stand and tug the skirt of my dress into place before hammering on the wall as I had intended to do in the first place. I can hear him fumbling and the quiet metal of his zipper then the shocked gasp as the panel in the desk pops open. "Don't even think it. Your daddy promised this to me a long time ago. Go ask him. And his left eyelid twitches when he lies." My purse is more than ample to carry the contents.

They have changed over the years; less bejeweled pretty things. to my regret, but much more cash and several bonds. The only thing that didn't make sense was the key in the bottle and I took it anyway.

"Junie? I don't know where she is. Victor took her out of here after Dad killed Asher. I'm sorry, for what it's worth. I liked him." I didn't expect an answer at all and my hand freezes over the opening of my bag. Victor was a spoiled, well lawyered and court determined non compos mentis, certifiably nuts. My poor baby.

"Why should I believe you? You stood there and watched him do it. Your mother told me how your father laughed like a child when he told her about it," I said quietly. I meant it to sting, to cut him with my knowledge but my voice can't carry the weight of my disappointment or of my hurt. The tiny clink of the bottle and key seems so final in this tight space and I really don't want to be in here with him anymore.

"I'm going to kill your parents. Both of them once I get some answers. I'm giving you until dark to make arrangements for your children, Tiff and yourself." My purse is heavier than I expect and I stagger a bit when I stand. "June, for fuck sake, will you listen to me? I didn't have time to say anything let alone move. Asher was telling Dad that he was taking you away, his new job came with a promotion and a move; he told Dad how he planned to surprise you with it when you got home that night when I walked into the office. I was shocked to see him there and Dad pulled that old revolver that he said didn't work from under his desk.

He was gone before I could do anything."

Promotion? A move away from here and freedom? More of the thievery that has plagued my life because of Timmy Kartish. "Is this where Asher's brains stuck to the wall Timmy?" I scream, slapping my palm on the new paneling, "Here? Or here?" The tears escape when I'd fought so hard to keep them trapped. Then his arms are around me and he is speaking rapidly in my ear, begging me to listen and understand.

"And you let your brother take our daughter, knowing what he was. Let me go Timmy. You have your family to attend to and I have a job to finish." His arms fall from around me and take the little warmth I had felt in forever with them.

Olivia is shouting in the lobby and her voice echoes back to where we stand still close but separated by the elephant in the room.

"This is the last chance I'm giving you," I offer, pausing in the doorway with my back to the room, "Where is my daughter? Where did Victor bury her? I have a right to know." There is no response other than the tired sigh of a man tired of talking and I leave him there in the room where Asher died with the knowledge that the deaths of his parents were on his head.

Tiffani had been a blabbermouth cunt who had forced me to react impulsively and I would not make the same mistake again. Olivia looks up at me with suspicious eyes when I re-enter the lobby with my purse now noticeably full and my eyes noticeably dry.

Pops' head turns back towards me with cold eyes and his hands clutching his seeping leg with an angry glare. "I've given your son two chances to give me the information I want. He has refused. I'm asking you Daddy-o, one spin all or nothing. Where is my daughter?"

Patriarch Pete's eyes slip to half mast, and glaze over slightly and this will not do. I place the barrel of the gun to Olivia's forehead, pressing hard between her eyes and raise my eyebrows at him in question.

"June don't do this. I told you no one knows where your little girl is, but I will help you find her if you just fucking stop this."

Timmy is standing behind me and his touch is chilly on the nape of my neck and not at all gentle. That motherfucker found the gun in his father's desk drawer. "Olivia, how about you? It doesn't matter if he blows my head off right now, you will still die. My finger is on the trigger and you have ten seconds to tell me something I can use."

The old woman glances at Pete in disgust and shakes her head before meeting my insistent stare. "The key in the bottle that was in his not so secret stash. Victor took her to the summer house where she would be safe and she is with the nanny I hired to keep her safe." The breath I didn't know I had been holding exploded from my chest in relief and dismay.

The firm pressure of cold steel faded away from my neck and mine didn't move an inch. The old bitch started to laugh, slapping her hand against Pop's chest as though he had told the funniest joke of his life, then sobered slightly to spit at her, "Did you really think we would let you keep her June? Asher wasn't her father; we introduced you to him so that it wouldn't look improper while Timmy got his shit together. I'm sure that Victor had some fun with her before he came home again."

Pops still hadn't moved and watched her through his slitted eyelids, his pallor waxy and lax. The old fuck slipped away while we weren't watching. Timmy is beside me, his father's gun in his hand pointed at the ground.

"Is it true June?" I had no designs to ever tell him that Dexie was his daughter, but his mother had destroyed that plan in short order. I nod and put a little more pressure on the trigger. "They threatened me the second they found out.

The day you fucked off and abandoned me for greener pastures or a younger snatch I found out that I was pregnant. That dinner you were supposed to show up for? Surprise! It's a girl."

He is watching me staring down the barrel into his mother's eyes and my hand shaking with the weight. Timmy's hand is on my neck and I flick my eyes away and out into the parking lot. The noise is incredible and I stand open mouthed and stunned. Olivia sways a moment with her hands at her throat and falls heavily to the floor. Timmy throws onto the cooling body of his father and walks out the front door and into the midst of those fucking idjits they gave weapons to.

The last letter that I had received before Asher had come into this den of iniquity to announce his plans came on bank letterhead and was attached to a thick stack of papers. Dexie was a year old then, and Timmy had just moved back to town with Tiffani and their two kids in tow. The letter stated that I was to sign them forthwith and prepare for a representative of the family to my daughter the following Friday or they would be sure that legal action was taken to me unfit. That was the end.

I glance down at the crumpled and sweat thinned piece of paper I had pulled from my bra cup; it is clutched in my hand and I am crushing it further as I pretend it's the trigger I am depressing then toss it down between the bodies.

Chief Sawton is speaking animatedly with Timmy, waving his pudgy hands around excitedly and grabbing his balding pate with his hands in frustration when Timmy shakes his head resignedly. Looping the strap of my purse across my middle, I snap a new magazine into the gun and push the glass-less door frame open, taking aim at the three buffoons closest to me and drop them all before they can draw their own weapons. The world stops making sounds as I pull the trigger again and again, the bodies falling like boneless bloodied sacks to the ground.

The two ogling the slut who had scratched my car look over surprised and the expression doesn't fade as they collapse to the ground to lie in their brains and blood.

The crowd is now running amok now, milling in a roiling mass of confusion and fear and the perfect cover for me. My high heel shoes click on the pavement, adding their odd percussion to the din, and it is all I can hear over the steady beating of my heart. I spy the Chief waddling as quickly as he can between the parked vehicles; Sweat is dripping from under his cap, making him shine in the sun like a suckling pig.

All around me people are calling out for others

and in one case, standing stock still and howling with her hands over her ears. That snatch who scratched my car. Her eyes are closed tight, clamped so tight in fact that her eyes are wrinkled at the corners; they pop open when the cold steel of my gun settles on her third eye with childlike wonder. With relish, I cock the hammer and smile sweetly, snarling, "You scratched my car."

She shakes her head slowly back and forth with her hand on the keys that still hang from her belt loop. She wobbles on those too high heels in fear, and I observe with amusement the dark stain spreading from her crotch.

I see Chief Sawton in my peripheral vision, his hands on his weapon and hear the click of the hammer. Son of a bitch, he is a sneaky bastard and I give him credit for cleverness. I begin to lower the gun and see the girl fall to her knees and watch while the first tears fall into her impressive cleavage.

I want to die, watching the child sobbing on the ground makes me deeply sad for her, and for her parents. The explosion so close to me startles me out of my reverie and I brace for the burn of a bullet, actually tired of this bullshit. When the burn doesn't come, I turn breathless to see Timmy walking toward the two remaining officers with a smile as he pulls the trigger again and again. I was so sure he had run.

"Junie, be a good girl now and drop the gun. Haven't you done enough?" Sweet Jesus, I had let Chief Sawton get behind me and I feel that tickle itch of a weapon trained between my shoulder blades. It's my own fault for becoming lost in the distraction. Dexie is the only thing on my mind when his clammy hand is on my wrist and the cold metal of handcuffs. What an idiot he is, not to disarm me first.

All around us is a ballet of terror, the unifying or perhaps quantifying emotion that brings all these people together is fear; I caused it. Timmy watches nearby, the left edge of his lip lifting up and down.

"Chief? You are truly a buffoon. It's a wonder you are able to dress yourself in the morning," I laugh, turning on my heel into his surprised face, "Goodbye." There would be no dancing for him as there had been for Victor. In fact, I am sure that several of his colleagues and his wife would vomit on first sight. His surprisingly delicate fingers play a mindless tune on the pavement with his feet keeping time in an oddly fitting end.

Standing over the body of the man I had essentially hobbled, his left knee missing from the knee and still leaking, I survey the melee. Tommy is standing next to me now, urging me to finish this one so we can get out of here and to Dexie and my heart leaps at the thought of my baby girl in my arms again.

The slut who scratched my car is still on her knees, still staring at me with tears staining her cheeks with the remnants of her too thick eye makeup, her eyes flickering between the legless man at my feet and his face as he looks up my skirt with wide eyed interest. Somethings never change and I am getting tired of hearing his bitching.

A squealing sound from the nearby road snaps my attention back to reality and I hand Timmy the purse and the keys. "Go get the car." He grabs my bag and runs, the keys jingling merrily in his fist.

Below me, the man that had been enjoying the free show runs his cruor streaked hand up my inner thigh, as I raise my own, pistol in hand and trained on the woman cop that has sped into the parking lot. Several people jump out of the way, staring opened mouthed at the car before running off again.

My last bullet takes the woman cop in the throat, effectively stopping her from sending one of hers into my skull. Her head explodes from her neck and bounces off the still flashing cherries on the top of her car where it splits apart in bits of mealy pink mush and bright scarlet. She stands for a moment, her body, then crumples into a heap under the open door. Damp from the excitement, and from my efforts. I can feel the cop's hand on my thigh, the fingers straining towards what he wishes he could have. He is muttering low, his mouth opening and closing in soundless words. Dropping to my knees, I settle my ass on his heaving chest and feel his lungs struggle to breathe under my weight, negligible though it is. "Please," he rasps and I stroke his cheek gently, while pulling the small, exquisitely sharp blade from my garter.

Timmy is honking the horn, two beeps then a longer, more impatient blast. Sensuously I touch the boy in blue, taking the time to reach my hand back to feel the size of his package. I wish I could save him for a time, but that is impossible. Dexie. Her name beats in my heart and in my veins. Gently wrapping my fingers in his hair, I force his neck back and slide my blade through the soft meat of his throat. He bucks under me, his hands slipping in the gush of hot read fluid that coats me and it smells richly of salted copper and sulfur.

"Come on June! This is no time to play," Timmy calls from the driver's seat of my 'Cuda with an indulgent smile, and he leans over to open the door for me. Rising to my feet, I point to the girl with a savage smile and she her recoil. Good. My car smells of Dexie, her sweet clean scent transporting me to where I hoped she was playing in the surf and laughing. Timmy squeezes my crimson gloved hand and puts the pedal to the floor.

Three days later

The sun is rising over the ocean, turning it from a dark abyss into a firestorm and we are sitting in the driveway of a well maintained home on the edge of the water, Timmy's arm around my waist and me shivering. We travelled without stopping, short of bathroom breaks and to gas up. I cleaned up in the bathroom on our first stop, nearly gagging from the reek of old blood.

There wasn't a lot I could do about my hair except rinse it in the filthy sink, and I watched the water flush out red for what felt like hours before it became a faded pink. Still, I felt more human in clean clothes and washed down. Timmy was waiting with the door open and two coffees in the console. My Hero.

I jumped out of the car the second it was safe enough to do so, and ran for the water, pulling my clothes off in desperation. I could her him laughing when I tripped and fell face first into the salty warm heaven. It was a purge, a soul cleansing, and I sobbed while I swam.

I'm not a monster – I never have been. The fact that I murdered, in cold blood admittedly, nine human beings with families and friends who are likely outraged, doesn't make me bad.

Sometimes, I think, leaning against the man I love, we are too controlled. Sometimes it's the lack of action that drives us to react and so I count those casualties as those unavoidable. There are several less evil souls walking the earth this morning, and I am good with that.

"She will be up soon. Are you ready for that?" I murmur against his neck, bracing for a sudden change of heart and relaxing when he kisses my forehead. I can feel his smile. "Any regrets? Your mother..." Timmy looks me in the eye with dead seriousness and shakes his head gravely. "She wasn't my mother. That woman raised me, as you know, with an iron fist covered in diamonds, but she didn't love me. That she saved for Victor. My mother died, at birth my father said. I have no information to the contrary." The door behind us flies open and a woman calls out to Timmy with delight, and he turns from me in anticipation. "Junie, there she is. Can I go?" He doesn't wait for my answer and sprints up the stairs.

Timmy is laughing and I can see tears on his cheek when Dexie reaches out her little hand and grasps his finger, then holds her arms out to him. A new day and the new start to a life that should have been this way from the start. I mourn for Asher, my heart breaks for the man that was there for me when I was at my lowest and loved me for it. He became a father to Dexie before she was even born; he died needlessly for me and for Dexie. She will know about her other dad, as it should be.

I leave them to bond a moment and wander along the veranda to view the wide area of land we were on. We might be alright here, if there is a God, I hope he will look over us, and forgive me for my failures. It was all in the name of good. As for me, even as I join my little family and step inside the house that would be my home for however long we have together.

I worry that one day I will look out one of these windows to a yard full of police cars and know that should that day come, I will without regret, take every soul there to protect my family.

ABOUT THE AUTHOR

Melanie McCurdie is a Canadian based writer who resides in Calgary, Alberta and is blessed with two challenging boys. A Warrior Mom to Sam, aged 14 and DaveyB, aged 10, administrator with The Twisted Path Group, rabid supporter of Independent Film and Publications, and a horror junkie with a taste for words, and bloodsauce.

Made in the USA
Lexington, KY
20 May 2019